WRATH OF THE GODS

A James Acton Thriller

By J. Robert Kennedy

James Acton Thrillers
The Protocol
Brass Monkey
Broken Dove
The Templar's Relic
Flags of Sin
The Arab Fall
The Circle of Eight
The Venice Code
Pompeii's Ghosts
Amazon Burning
The Riddle
Blood Relics
Sins of the Titanic
Saint Peter's Soldiers
The Thirteenth Legion
Raging Sun
Wages of Sin
Wrath of the Gods

Special Agent Dylan Kane Thrillers
Rogue Operator
Containment Failure
Cold Warriors
Death to America
Black Widow

Delta Force Unleashed Thrillers
Payback
Infidels
The Lazarus Moment
Kill Chain
Forgotten

Detective Shakespeare Mysteries
Depraved Difference
Tick Tock
The Redeemer

Zander Varga, Vampire Detective
The Turned

WRATH OF THE GODS

A James Acton Thriller

J. ROBERT KENNEDY

Copyright © 2017 J. Robert Kennedy

CreateSpace

All rights reserved. No part of this publication may be reproduced, stored in or introduced into a retrieval system, or transmitted in any form, or by any means (electronic, mechanical, photocopying, recording or otherwise) without the prior written permission of the publisher.

This is a work of fiction. Names, characters, places, and incidents are products of the author's imagination. Any resemblance to actual persons, living or dead, is entirely coincidental.

ISBN-10: 1544076061

ISBN-13: 978-1544076065

First Edition

10 9 8 7 6 5 4 3 2 1

For the over 100,000 dead from the Mexican war on drugs.
And the over 27,000 missing.

WRATH OF THE GODS

A James Acton Thriller

"Having received the Mandate from Heaven, may (the emperor) lead a long and prosperous life." (**受命於天，既壽永昌**)

Inscription by Prime Minister Li Si on the Heirloom Seal of the Realm, circa 221 BC

"We're all afraid in Mexico now. We can't let fear beat us."

Marisol Valles García
Former 21-year-old police chief of Praxedis G. Guerrero, Mexico, forced to flee to the United States after months of threats from the drug cartels.

PREFACE

There is a story that when Columbus arrived in America, the natives couldn't see his ships, as their minds couldn't perceive them, the concept of vessels so large, simply too much for them to comprehend. This has been largely dismissed as ridiculous, the very idea that large ships could park offshore and not be noticed for hours or days, laughable.

Yet dismissing this idea out of hand would be premature. There is evidence to suggest that the natives saw the boats, yet simply had no concept as to what they were looking at, therefore didn't see them as boats, but something else entirely.

Or nothing at all.

A mirage.

And it has been suggested these sightings—or lack thereof—weren't the first.

Legends, maps, and even pre-Columbian writings bearing a remarkable resemblance to ancient Chinese, have been found, suggesting the Chinese visited the Americas long before Columbus.

Yet if this were true, shouldn't there be some evidence left behind? Some tangible proof that the Chinese had actually arrived?

Of course, there wouldn't be, if that evidence were intentionally erased.

Pacific Coastal Region
Maya Highlands, Maya Empire
1092 AD

Balam Canek stared at the sea, the waves roaring against the shore, the water extending out into the distance, lost to the sun low on the horizon. Something was wrong. Something was different. He couldn't put his finger on it, what it could be, though something was definitely not right.

"What is it?"

He glanced at his wife, Nelli. "I'm not sure. Do you see something? On the water?"

She stared, squinting into the sun, then shook her head. "No, nothing. Do you?"

He shrugged, holding his hand up to shield some of the light. "I don't know. Something isn't right. It's like a mirage. I know something is there, but I can't quite make it out."

Her eyes narrowed. "Where?"

He pointed directly ahead. "I think there's something there, but there can't be, right?"

She stepped toward the water, her bare feet leaving cute little indentations in the sand. He followed. "Was there ever an island there?"

He gave her a look. "We've lived here our entire lives. You know the answer to that."

She grunted. "Then I don't know what I see."

He grabbed onto the words. "But you *do* see something!"

She frowned, her head bobbing slowly. "Yes, there's definitely something there, but I have no idea what it is. It must be a trick. Perhaps Bitol is having fun with us?"

He chuckled at the reference to the Sky God. It could be. The gods were known to toy with their creations from time to time, or to show their displeasure. Sacrifices would be made over the coming days, he had no doubt. The gods would be appeased, and whatever this was, would go away.

Nelli gasped, jabbing a finger toward the sea. "Balam, look!"

He turned to where she was pointing and his jaw dropped. It was a boat, filled with perhaps ten men, men dressed as nothing he had ever seen. Suddenly everything came into focus, as if a great fog had lifted, though this was nothing physical, nothing natural, instead a fog of the mind as it made sense of what he had been staring at for so long. "May the gods protect us! I see it! It's a floating island!"

Nelli stared, her mouth agape, then she grabbed his arm, gripping it tight. "But it can't be! That's impossible!"

He didn't say anything, instead standing frozen in place, his entire body shaking as his heart hammered. It was an island, floating on the water, rising and falling with the waves. Yet it was more than that. There were at least half a dozen of the islands, all clustered together, giving the illusion from a distance of one massive creation. And now, several boats, loaded with strange men, strange creatures, sailed toward the shore, toward them.

"I-I've never seen anything like it! Who could create such a thing?"

Nelli tugged on his arm, trying to lead him away. "Come, we must go warn the others. Nothing good can possibly come of this."

He resisted at first, continuing to stare at the strange land floating upon the sea.

It must be the gods. And they must be angry!

"Balam! Come!"

The first boat hit the beach, its prow cutting into the sand, those aboard jumping over the sides. They appeared to be men, yet not. They had two arms and two legs, like himself, though their eyes were thin and slanted, unlike any he had ever seen.

Except in an animal, glowering in the dark.

He shivered. These were not men at all. They were covered in some sort of thick, rigid hide, like the scales of a reptile, one of them, obviously the leader, stepping onto the sand and saying something in a tongue he had not heard before, shimmering in the sunlight as if his skin were made of gold. One of them pointed in their direction. Something was shouted. Balam turned and grabbed Nelli by the hand, terror gripping his chest.

They must be here to punish us!

"We have to warn the others!"

Fairmont Mayakoba Resort

Riviera Maya, Mexico

Present Day

"Man, this is the life." Archaeology Professor James Acton held up his margarita and clinked glasses with his wife and love of his life, Archaeology Professor Laura Palmer.

"It is, indeed."

Acton swapped hands and presented his glass with salted rim to one of their best friends, Interpol Agent Hugh Reading. Reading eyed the ridiculously emasculating glass and tapped it with his own beer, in a bottle, that he had managed to have warmed to his own liking, everything at the exclusive resort chilled to North American expectations, not the cellar temperature his British heritage demanded. "Cheers."

"Cheers." Acton drained his drink then raised it high, a cabana boy rushing over.

"Another, señor?"

"Absolutely." The young boy smiled, taking the empty glass and turned to Laura who waved him off.

"No, love, I need my legs working later."

"Damn right you do."

"James!"

Reading snorted then drained his bottle, handing it to the boy. "It tastes like another."

"Right away, señor."

The boy rushed off, and Reading let out a loud sigh as he sank back in his lounge chair. "Did I thank you for inviting me?"

Laura winked at her husband. "Only a few dozen times."

Reading gave her a look. "Well, thank you again." He glanced at Acton. "Add it to the tally, I'm sure you're keeping score."

Acton grinned. "I just wish Greg could have come with the family."

"Back problems?"

Acton shook his head, thankful that wasn't the issue. His friend had been shot in the back several years ago, and initially, the doctors had thought he'd never walk again. Thankfully, they were wrong. Greg Milton could now walk, though his stamina was still a challenge, the pain eventually returning to the point where he'd have to sit down.

But walking was walking.

"Alumni problems. The state cut some of our funding, so he's trying to make up the difference."

"Is your job at risk?"

"He's my best friend. It better not be."

"Well, if it is, Professor Acton, perhaps you can come work with me."

Acton flinched then twisted around to see the source of the comment. And smiled. "Eduardo! What the hell are you doing here?" He stood, extending his hand, Eduardo Morales taking it and pulling him in for a thumping hug.

"My friend, I am delighted you are here! So much so, I will not chastise you for failing to tell me you were coming with your lovely wife."

Laura rose, giving Morales a hug. "Good to see you, Eduardo, it's been too long."

"Yes, the antiquities conference in Jordan." He motioned toward Acton. "Before this one found you and made an honest woman of you."

Laura grinned. "I like to think *I* made an honest *man* out of him."

Reading eyed the colorful margarita just arriving. "Are you sure you made a *man* out of him?"

Acton feigned a punch to Reading's midriff. "May I introduce our good friend, Hugh Reading of Interpol."

Morales shook Reading's hand. "A pleasure."

"Likewise." Reading took his beer, testing the temperature and giving the cabana boy a thumbs up. "Keep them coming like that, lad, and you'll have a good tip at the end of this." The boy beamed then rushed off to his next customer.

Acton gestured toward an empty chair under the large umbrella. "Take a load off and tell us what's new with you. Are you here on vacation?"

Morales sat then leaned forward, his elbows on his knees. "No, Jim, I'm here looking for you guys."

Acton's eyes narrowed. "Why?"

Morales leaned in closer, lowering his voice. "I've made a discovery, one so significant, I don't know who I can trust."

Pacific Coastal Region
Maya Highlands, Maya Empire
1092 AD

Cheng Jun steadied himself in the boat then leaped into the water as they reached shore. He and the others pulled the boat aground, careful to keep their feet in the water, for the honor of setting foot upon dry land would be that of their Admiral, Khong Hui. He had doubted they would ever see land again, yet here they were, on the shores of some strange, new world, a world none of his people had ever before seen. It was terrifying yet exciting, and it was truly an honor that he had been chosen to not only serve aboard the fleet's flagship, but to be part of the initial landing party. His family would never have believed it, and he just prayed that one day he'd see them again, so they could share in the honor this day should bring to his children and grandchildren, for generations to come.

For today was a great day.

They were here to spread the mighty Song Dynasty across the sea, to the lands long rumored to lie across the great ocean, and perhaps return with untold riches, a share every man in the crew had been assured of, should they do their duty.

And he had done his duty.

"I claim this land in the name of the Emperor, and the Song Dynasty!" Admiral Khong stepped from the prow and onto the beach, walking several paces inland, no one daring move until his boots touched the dry sand. Admiral Khong surveyed the area, his head held high, chin jutted forward, the air of superiority evident to all, a superiority well-deserved.

For he carried the great seal, the Heirloom Seal of the Realm, given to him by the Emperor himself, to prove his authority should it ever be challenged. Though here, in this desolate place, Cheng could imagine no one challenging the Empire, the Emperor, or his representative on this mission.

With a flick of the wrist, Admiral Khong ordered them forward, and Cheng, with the others, pulled the boat farther ashore then fanned out, forming a protective wedge in front of their leader. What strange beasts may be lurking in the thick forest ahead of them, he did not know, but he would happily sacrifice himself to its claws should it mean saving the life of Admiral Khong, and guaranteeing the security of his family for years to come. To die saving one's admiral was the dream of peasants like him, and though he hoped his armor would protect him so he might live to see his beloved wife and their three children again, his death would bring them far more.

Something moved to their left and he gasped, a man and woman, perhaps his age, were standing at the tree line, staring at them, almost naked. He pointed. "Sir!"

Route 295

Approaching Tepich, Mexico

Present Day

Professor James Acton held onto the doorframe—tight. Eduardo Morales not only had a lead foot, he also appeared to have an aversion for keeping his eyes on the road, every word spoken needing to be addressed with eye contact. Thankfully, he used the mirror for Laura in the back seat, Reading merely staring ahead, saying nothing, probably regretting his decision to join them.

"As you know, when the Spanish first arrived, they burned all of the Mayan books they could find, considering them blasphemous as they too often described the Mayan gods. Ybanez de Landa was particularly guilty of this, despite the fact he is responsible for most of what we know about the ancient Mayans."

Acton nodded. Ybanez de Landa had been a Spanish Franciscan monk, and had been responsible for burning almost all of the Mayan's written works—priceless, irreplaceable artifacts. Ancient texts, literature, manuals—the records of an advanced civilization—all destroyed by ignorance and arrogance. Until today, only four Mayan books were known to exist.

Until today.

"I've read his book of course, and copies of the four Mayan texts—the translations at least. My Mayan is rusty, but hers is excellent."

Morales spun in his seat, staring at Laura. "May I confess something?"

"You just might have to. We're about to die!" Morales glanced at Reading then spun around, swerving back onto the road. "How about I drive?" suggested Reading.

Morales laughed. "Not to worry, God, I think, is on our side today."

Reading frowned. "It's not God I'm worried about."

Laura playfully slapped him and leaned between the two front seats. "What is it that you have to confess?" Morales turned to face her, but she gently pushed his face back toward the road. "I must insist, otherwise my friend back here will either have a heart attack, or shoot you."

"I don't have my gun."

"Heart attack, then."

Morales laughed. "You'd never survive the streets of Mexico City if my driving bothers you!" He adjusted his mirror so he could see everyone in the rear seat. "My confession"—he glanced at Acton and gave him a rueful smile—"is that I actually came looking for you, Laura."

Acton's eyebrows rose. "I thought you said Greg told you where we were?"

"He did. I didn't know how to reach your wife, so called your university to ask. Dean Milton told me you were both here. I, umm, didn't want to hurt your feelings when you thought I came to find you."

Acton chuckled. "My feelings would have only been hurt if you were looking for him." He jabbed a thumb over his shoulder at Reading.

Reading grunted. "Nobody's ever looking for me."

Laura patted his knee. "Now, now, don't get grumpy."

"I'm hungry. We missed lunch. I'm going to be grumpy." Laura reached into her purse and handed him a protein bar. He brightened until he took his first bite. "What is this, chocolate flavored chalk?"

She gave him a look. "There's just no pleasing you today, is there?"

"No."

She handed him a bottle of water. "Here, this makes it go down easier."

Reading chewed as he unscrewed the cap then took a swig, saying nothing, apparently content enough. Laura turned her attention back to Morales. "So, you were saying?"

"I need an expert in Ancient Mayan, and that's you."

"Forgive me for saying, but that's you, too, isn't it? In fact, aren't you considered *the* Ancient Mayan expert?"

Morales bowed slightly, his head dipping below the dash, Reading's eyes bulging. "Some would say so, yes."

"*Most* would say so," said Acton, pointing at the road. "But, yes, my wife is definitely up there as well." He beamed a smile back at her with a wink.

"Thank you, dear."

He grinned. "You're welcome, dear."

"Ahh, new love. I remember when I felt the same way about my wife."

"Eduardo! You don't love your wife anymore?"

"Oh! No no no no no! I love her very much, it's just different after twenty years of marriage. You don't show it as much."

"And you aren't so quick to show it in front of others."

Laura slapped Reading again as Acton unbuckled his seatbelt and turned around. "I'm coming back there to make love to my wife. Object?"

"Bloody hell!"

Acton roared with laughter, returning to his seat and strapping back in. He glanced at Morales, still laughing. "So you needed a second opinion on what you found?"

"Yes."

"But I thought you found a lost Mayan library? Surely you don't need Laura to confirm that?"

Morales shook his head. "It's not the library that concerns me, it's what else we found in the library."

Acton's eyes narrowed, the excitement in Morales' tone palpable. "What did you find?"

"Something that changes everything."

Pacific Coastal Region
Maya Highlands, Maya Empire
1092 AD

Balam Canek rushed through the dense forest, one hand extended in front of him as he pushed the thick brush aside, the other tightly gripping Nelli. His heart slammed hard as he tried to make sense of what he had seen. A giant floating island, regurgitating strange men onto the sea as if some portal to another world had opened, unleashing demonic minions into their peaceful existence as punishment for something, something they must have done, something that the human sacrifices were no longer enough to satisfy.

But what could it be?

He had heard about the great drought, though its effects hadn't been felt by his people, at least not yet. They had taken in refugees over the years, those who had fled the devastation rather than hold out and trust that the priests and shamans would save them. They were the cowards, the unfaithful. To abandon one's home and family in the face of adversity was shameful, which was why those welcomed into the village lived a lonely life on the outskirts.

Tolerated, and not much more.

Balam and Nelli reached them first.

One of the refugees rushed up to him, concern on his face. "Balam, what's wrong?"

He came to a halt, gasping to catch his breath, Nelli doing the same beside him, and though he felt safer now that his home was in sight, he feared there would be no safe place from the creatures now arriving. "Something's happened. Something terrible."

The man's formidable muscles tensed. "What?"

"A great darkness has arrived. Strange men. Strange creatures. Coming forth from the belly of a beast so large, it can only have been sent by the gods."

Others had gathered, the fear in their eyes mounting, Balam growing more terrified with each word that came out of his mouth, for it couldn't have been an island. Islands didn't float. It had to be a creature of the sea, a creature so massive it was unfathomable to even consider the power wielded to create such a thing.

They were doomed.

"I need to see the Chief." He grabbed Nelli's hand. "We must raise a war party! We must prepare to fight!"

The newcomers sprang into action, the men rushing to their homes as Balam led Nelli deeper into the village, the refugees emerging with weapons, prepared to defend their new home. Balam looked at his friend, Kawil, a newcomer who had been here for as long as he could remember, still not fully accepted into the village, the diaspora from the drought-ravaged areas, no matter how long ago their arrival, forever relegated to the fringe of society.

Yet not Kawil.

For some reason, they had become friends, though it was a friendship of the forest lest the others find out and ostracize him as well. A nod was exchanged, and little else. And his chest ached with the knowledge they could never truly be friends. Though after today, it might not matter, should the wrath of the gods be unleashed upon them.

He spotted the Chief in the center of the village, congregating with several of the elders. "Chief! I must speak with you!"

A hand was held up, and nothing more, one of the elders talking.

"The well is as low as I've ever seen it."

The Chief waved his hand. "But look about. I see no signs of drought."

"It's the river. Its banks are showing like never before. Its source is to the east, where we know the drought has taken hold. It's only a matter of time before we too are affected."

Balam bit his tongue as he waited impatiently for his chance to speak, interrupting the Chief and the elders, something that just wasn't done.

"What would you have me do?"

No answers appeared forthcoming until the priest finally spoke. "The gods must be displeased." He motioned toward where they had just come, toward the settlement of newcomers. "Perhaps it is because we tolerate those who would show their lack of faith by abandoning their homes and their gods so easily."

Heads bobbed, and Balam's chest tightened as he realized what was about to be proposed.

"We should banish them immediately. Perhaps then the gods will be satisfied, and spare us this curse."

More bobbing heads.

"Forgive me for interrupting, but—"

The hand rose again, and this time was accompanied by a glare, a glare that caused Balam to shrink away like it had since he was a boy.

"Things have become worse with the latest arrivals, and more seem to be coming every day as word spreads of our generosity. I have always felt that the gods wished us to show mercy to our fellow man, however *I* am just a man, and perhaps have been mistaken." The Chief sighed. "Perhaps my generosity has been misplaced. It was one thing to willingly share what little we have with a few, but the few have turned into many, into a flood, and that flood threatens to overwhelm us. Even if the gods are not punishing us for our misplaced generosity, we nonetheless suffer because of it. There are only so many crops, so many fish in the river, so many animals to feed and clothe us, and now this." He motioned at the communal well. "I think we have made a mistake by letting these people stay." He squared his shoulders, and Balam's stomach flipped as the words he had dreaded for years were uttered. "Let it be known, that from this day forth, no one not born to this village will be welcome here unless it is through marriage." He turned toward the newcomers' encampment. "They leave, today." Murmurs of assent grew from the others gathered. "And choose one for a sacrifice. We must appease the gods for our arrogance."

Applause and cheers erupted, and soon the gathered men left, reappearing with their spears and axes, marching toward the edge of the village to deliver the news and choose their victim.

Balam felt sick, his purpose forgotten.

"What is it, Balam? What is it that has you so flustered?"

Balam stared at the Chief for a moment, his mind blank. Nelli elbowed him.

"Balam!"

He glanced at her, the urgency in her eyes finally reminding him. "Demons! On the beach!"

The Chief's eyes narrowed. "What are you talking about?"

"We saw them, dozens if not more, landing on the shore, coming from some huge, floating island or creature."

The Chief stared at him, a slight smile finally breaking out. "You were always the joker, boy. Like your mother."

Nelli stepped forward. "He's not joking, sir, it's true. I saw it with my own eyes. Strange creatures, standing on two feet like us, but covered in thick scales with narrow, slanted…*evil* eyes."

The Chief stared at Nelli, his smile gone. "You two are being serious, aren't you?"

Balam nodded furiously. "Yes. And there isn't much time. More were coming."

The Chief grasped at his temples, pushing against them as if battling a fierce headache. "If these are indeed demons, then they must be from the realm of the gods." He glanced at the priest. "What do you think, holy one?"

The priest gestured at the well. "We have already seen the anger of the gods, and this lack of water was just a warning. It has been going on for over a year, and we have done nothing to heed it. Just this week we took in three more who have turned their backs on the gods. Perhaps these demons are our punishment for not listening."

The Chief turned toward the edge of the village where screams and cries could be heard from the newcomers as the men of the village emptied their homes, some as well-built as any in the village, others makeshift shelters for those who had not yet committed to staying permanently. "Will ridding ourselves of them appease the gods?"

The priest shook his head. "I fear it may not. We may yet need to pay a price in blood."

"Then a sacrifice?"

"Yes, but one of our own. It is hardly punishment to kill an outsider."

The Chief sighed, closing his eyes. "I refuse to believe the gods would punish us for doing a good deed. These people may have turned their backs on their homes, but they pray as we all do, participate in all the rituals. I see no evidence beyond doing whatever it took to save their families, that these people have any less faith in the gods than you or I." The priest recoiled as if physically wounded by the words. The Chief recognized the perceived insult and reached out, gripping the elderly man's shoulder. "I, of course, should have excluded you. None have more faith than you."

This appeased the priest. "Then a sacrifice it is?"

The Chief shook his head as he watched a young man race by with a bowl of blue paint. A scream erupted, a scream Balam recognized only too well—it was his friend, Kawil. Two villagers were dragging him toward the square, Kawil kicking and screaming as he realized what was happening, the blue paint used for only one thing.

To mark those about to be sacrificed, the blue color chosen to honor the rain gods.

Tears welled in Balam's eyes as he stared at his friend. He spun to the Chief. "Sir, please, not him."

The Chief patted him on the shoulder. "There will be no sacrifice today." He stepped forward, raising his hands. Everyone fell silent, only Kawil's whimpers breaking the hush. "Raise a war party! We must go to the beaches and meet these messengers of the gods and convince them that we have repented!"

The priest, his voice low, stepped closer. "And should they not listen?"

"Then the price in blood will be paid by both sides."

Universidad Veracruzana Archaeological Site
South of Tepich, Mexico
Present Day

James Acton pushed through the trees and gasped as he stepped into a large clearing, half a dozen members of Professor Morales' team hard at work on what was a stone entranceway embedded in the side of a hill.

And he felt a little disappointed.

"I thought you said it was huge? The hill doesn't look that big."

Morales slapped him on the back, urging him forward. "My friend, this is nothing. The tip of the proverbial iceberg. They buried it underground."

As they approached the entrance, Laura surged ahead, taking out her phone and recording the hieroglyphs surrounding the archway.

"What does it say?" asked Acton as Reading stepped up beside him, looking much the worse for wear. Acton picked several burrs off the poor man and flicked a millipede he clearly wasn't aware of, off his shoulder.

Laura traced her hand along the archway, pointing at each symbol as she went along. "Roughly, it says, 'Here lies the wealth of knowledge shared by the gods, preserved lest the wrath of the new arrivals from the west prevail.'" She stepped back, running over it again, mumbling the words. She turned to Morales. "Am I right?"

He shook his head, smiling. "It took me hours to be sure, but yes." He pointed at one of the hieroglyphs. "You said 'new arrivals from the west' here, and not just 'new arrivals.' Why?"

Laura stepped closer, pointing at the stone in question. "See the slight indentation in the symbol on the left-hand side. There was something here, but it's eroded over time. I'm assuming it was the sun, and based on its position, it was indicating the sun in the western sky."

Morales' jaw dropped. "Of course!" He stepped back, rereading the symbols to himself, tapping his chin rapidly. "Very strange."

Reading picked a stray bug from his hair. "Why? We know the Spanish arrived here and destroyed the Mayans. So they built a library to protect their knowledge."

Acton shook his head. "You're missing the key word."

"What's that?"

"West."

Reading shrugged. "Yeah, so? The west. The Western world. Heard of it?"

Acton grinned. "Yes, *we* have, but how would they? 'The West' is a modern day term. And for them, Columbus and those who followed came from the *east*, not the *west*. It's the wrong ocean. If the new arrivals they are referring to came from the west, then that's the Pacific Ocean, not the Atlantic."

Reading paused, his eyebrows slowly rising. "Oh." His eyes widened. "Oh!" They narrowed. "Then who the bloody hell are they talking about?"

Morales smiled. "I have something to show you that just might answer your question."

Pacific Coastal Region
Maya Highlands, Maya Empire
1092 AD

Cheng Jun stood near the edge of the forest, his eyes peering into the darkness of the thick trees, seeing nothing but shadows, the creatures living within, loudly protesting their arrival. He glanced over his shoulder as orders were shouted, over one hundred now ashore, supplies of food, water, and weapons quickly accumulating on the beach. Admiral Khong had ordered a camp to be set up and scouting parties deployed to search for fresh food and water, and any sign of civilization. They had seen two people already, a young man and woman, though they had appeared primitive, like those they had found on several islands in the ocean, there little wealth among those so unsophisticated living surrounded by water.

Yet this land appeared vast, stretching for as far as the eye could see, and they had sailed along its coast for days without any signs of manmade structures. There were no boats, no ports, no cities. But today, he had heard shouts from the others of wisps of smoke, perhaps campfires, the first sign of people.

And where there were people, there could be treasure.

A shiver ran up his spine at the thought. What gold and jewels could these people have? He feared little, what with the fact those he had seen had no jewelry to speak of, instead wearing barely anything.

And such strange people.

Their foreheads appeared broad and flat, unlike anything he had ever seen. In his travels, he had witnessed all manner of people, people of different skin colors, heights, weights, and mannerisms, tattooed, pierced, and bejeweled. He had even seen one man with massive earlobes, something he had apparently done to himself. But flat foreheads he had never before encountered.

Perhaps they're not human like us.

He dismissed the thought as ridiculous. They were human, though clearly primitive. But a tiger was primitive yet deadly, and these people could be as well. He gripped the hilt of his sword a little tighter as something moved in the trees.

"Somebody's coming!" He stepped back several paces as he drew his sword, the others around him doing the same, creating a protective circle around Admiral Khong. A bead of sweat ran down his back, causing him to shiver, sounds of rage erupting from the forest in front of them as what seemed like an army of angry souls prepared to confront them.

This isn't going to end well.

Universidad Veracruzana Archaeological Site
South of Tepich, Mexico
Present Day

James Acton followed Eduardo Morales down a spiraling staircase, perfectly preserved, lights running along the floor powered by solar panels outside. If it weren't for the smell of an environment closed in for hundreds of years, he might think he were at any number of well-known archaeological sites in this hemisphere.

While the world had been enamored by the Egyptian pyramids for centuries, the equally impressive structures of the Mesoamerican civilizations, built by the mighty empires of the Incan, Aztec and Mayan cultures, seemed an afterthought to those outside his field of study. These empires had existed for thousands of years, had rich histories of scientific advancement and cultural accomplishments, yet perhaps because there was little left beyond the structures themselves, they seemed forgotten.

Their treasures and art were looted by the Spanish, much of it melted down for their gold and jewels, whereas the Egyptian treasures, while looted, were at least preserved, and many today returned to their rightful owners, the Egyptian people. Sadly, with much if not most of the ancient cultures of the Americas, there was nothing left to return.

But as he rounded the final bend in the stairs, he gasped, all the wonder of a forgotten, ignored era, restored, a pristine, untouched treasure-trove of culture and art, laid out before them, had him frozen in place.

"Oh my God, James, it's…it's beautiful!"

Acton stood, slack-jawed at the sight before him. It was indeed a library, but much more. It appeared to be a museum, designed to preserve a culture that knew it was in danger of being destroyed. "How big is it?" he finally managed to ask Morales as his legs at last unlocked and he ventured deeper into the large chamber.

"Four rooms like this, all filled like this." Morales pointed at the far wall, stacked high with piles of bark paper coated with lime. "Each room contains hundreds of pages like this. We've examined only a few—they are very fragile. We'll have to extract each one and properly scan them, but we're already learning so much." He paused, his voice cracking. "It's the discovery of a lifetime."

Acton put an arm around his friend's shoulders and gave him a squeeze. "You'll go down in history for this one, my friend. Just as Carter is remembered for Tut, you'll be remembered for returning the Mayan culture to the world."

Morales smiled and wiped a tear from the corner of his eye. "Thank you, Jim, thank you." He inhaled loudly through his nose and held it for a moment, regaining his composure. "Every time I step in here, I'm overwhelmed." He pointed to an archway to their right. "But there's something in there that is even more significant than all this."

Acton took Laura's hand and followed Morales into another chamber, wondering what could possibly be more spectacular than what he had already seen. Morales strode to the middle of the room, blocking their view of some sort of table or altar. He turned, smiling.

"Over one thousand years of history have been rewritten here today."

He stepped aside, and Acton's eyes bulged as Laura gasped beside him.

"But that's impossible!"

Pacific Coastal Region
Maya Highlands, Maya Empire
1092 AD

Balam Canek stopped near the edge of the forest, the sun low on the horizon, reaching only a few paces ahead of him. The others formed a haphazard line along the day's edge, these new arrivals now numbering in the hundreds, their strange skin and heads casting long, terrifying shadows across the sand as the surf continued to crash rhythmically behind them as if urging them deeper ashore.

"You see? I told you they were demons!"

The Chief nodded, his eyes wide with fear, something Balam had never seen in the old man before. It sent a chill through his entire body, and he gripped his spear tighter, his palms slick with sweat.

"What are we going to do?"

The Chief inhaled deeply and squared his shoulders, the courage Balam was accustomed to seeing, returning. "We will not suffer these demons without a fight." The elderly priest arrived and peered through the trees. His eyes narrowed as he took in the sight before them. "What manner of creatures are these?" asked the Chief. "Have you seen their kind before?"

"Only in my nightmares. They are indeed sent by the gods."

Some of the courage vacated the Chief's face. "But are *they* gods?"

The priest shook his head. "No, none that I recognize."

"But how would you know?" cried Balam. "Have you met the gods?"

The priest glared at him.

"Balam! Watch your tongue!"

Balam bowed his head at the Chief's rebuke. "I'm sorry, I'm just…"

"You're scared, I know, we all are, but this is no reason to lose control over one's mouth." The Chief turned to the priest. "Would you recognize a god that has our best interests at heart?"

"Of course."

"Then if you don't recognize these creatures, then either they are not gods, or they are gods we do not worship. Am I right?"

"I believe you are."

"Then they must leave, or die."

Balam lifted his head slightly, staring up at the two elders. "But what if they *have* been sent by our gods? Would not attacking them displease them?"

"The gods use their powers to control our fates and the elements that surround us. They provide us with sunlight, rain, and abundant crops when they are pleased, or cloud the skies, let our wells run dry, or plague our crops, when they are not. Never do they send demons to our shores to punish us. These creatures are not from our gods, of that, I can assure you, though they may be rivals to our gods."

The Chief's eyebrows rose. "Rivals to our gods? That is an interesting proposition. Then fighting them would please our gods."

"Absolutely."

"But it could come at a high price." The Chief held out his hands, quelling the angry shouts challenging the newcomers, the scores of men now lining the forest's edge, turning to their leader. "I will go speak to them and tell them they are not welcome. Do nothing unless I say so." The Chief stepped forward and Balam grabbed his arm.

"And should they kill you?"

The Chief patted Balam's hand. "Then you will become chief, my son, and the decision will be yours."

Balam gulped, swallowing the lump that had formed in his throat. It had been years since his father had acknowledged him as his son, and an equal number of years since he had stopped thinking of the man as such. Tradition dictated the chief was the father to all once he took his station. He lived with his new wife, the daughter of a neighboring chief, communing with the elders and their gods, though Balam knew his mother on occasion still visited his father in the night.

He thought of Nelli, and how he would have to give her up should he become chief. The very idea filled him with sorrow.

I could never give her up.

And he was too young to be chief. He had yet to have any children, therefore had no heir. Could he refuse the position? He wasn't certain. He had never heard of anyone doing so before. It had never been a desire of his to rule—he had figured in time he would come to embrace his destiny, yet not today, not in the next few minutes.

He glanced down at the cloth bracelet Nelli had made him when they first declared their love for each other, and his chest ached.

Maybe I can change the law. Maybe when I am chief, I can declare an end to the tradition of giving up your family.

The Chief, his father, pulled his arm free, their eyes meeting, his love and fear evident.

He knows he's going to die.

"I will come with you, father."

His father shook his head. "No, son. You must stay here in case something happens." He turned and stepped onto the beach, striding confidently toward the large group of demons that had formed a line between them and what appeared to be their leader, a man adorned in black and gold, who to Balam had every appearance of a god. He watched his father, fear and pride welling within his heart.

His father raised his spear over his head. "I am Votan, and by the authority handed to me by my ancestors, I alone am responsible for these shores. If you come in peace, then I welcome you, but should you come to punish us, then know this—we will resist. If you truly are sent by our gods, then know that we have banished those who had lost faith, and accept our punishment—the warning of drought has been received, and we thank you for your guidance and assistance in returning us to the correct path you have laid out for us. No further action on your part is necessary."

There was a pause, then the demons separated, leaving an opening. Their leader stepped through, saying something, his voice loud, strong, yet uttering words unlike any Balam had ever heard. And they sounded menacing. His father shook his spear at the creature.

"You have heard my words! You are not of this realm, and I command you to leave us in peace! Leave us, or you shall feel the wrath of our gods as they exact their vengeance upon you should you harm their loyal subjects!"

The demon shouted something in response. Clearly, there was no understanding of what his father was saying. He glanced at the priest, this development lending credence to what he had said. Surely anyone sent by their gods would understand their language? He prayed that he was correct, for should he be wrong, they might be about to start a war between the gods and the Mayan people.

A war they had no possible hope of winning.

Universidad Veracruzana Archaeological Site
South of Tepich, Mexico
Present Day

"But this is Chinese!"

James Acton rushed forward, reaching out but resisting the urge to touch the imperial armor that sat behind the table, mounted to a stone sculpture of a man, the regalia impressive and perfectly preserved.

"It's tenth or eleventh century, I believe, Song Dynasty?"

Acton nodded, agreeing with Laura's assessment. "It's beautiful. Clearly the armor of a leader." He turned to Morales. "But how? How could this be here? Shipwreck?" He thought of Lord Richard Baxter, a prominent member of the Triarii, whose body had been found by his team in Peru, dating back to the thirteenth century.

America had been discovered long before Columbus, the Vikings the most prominent, having settled Iceland then Greenland and Newfoundland during the centuries-long Medieval Warm Period. They farmed the now barren soils of Greenland for centuries, growing corn and barley, before the natural global warming gave way to the Little Ice Age that lasted almost five hundred years, during which the Thames River in London would completely freeze, and revelers celebrating the Frost Fair would skate its length.

There was even some evidence to suggest the Chinese may have arrived here centuries ago, before Columbus, though there had never been any concrete evidence like this. A full suit of perfectly preserved Chinese imperial armor.

Laura gasped beside him, and he turned to see what she was staring at. His eyes followed hers then he gasped as well. "Oh my God, is that what I think it is?"

Morales smiled. "I don't want to sound the fool, so why don't you tell me what *you* think it is?"

Acton stepped forward and carefully picked up the small, green ornament, turning it gently in his hands, the block of jade heavy, intricately carved with a detailed coiled dragon on the top, several Chinese symbols on the bottom, and an inscription surrounding the base. He held it out for Laura, his eyes wide, his heart pounding, her own mouth agape in awe.

"It can't be!"

"I know, right!"

"What the bloody hell is it?"

Acton glanced over at the forgotten Reading. "It's the Heirloom Seal of the Realm, the Chinese imperial seal, lost one thousand years ago during the Song Dynasty."

"Okay, so it's some old Chinese thing. What's its significance?"

Acton returned his stare to the priceless artifact. "It's sort of like the Crown Jewels of your monarchy. It's essentially the proof that you are the emperor, or acting on his behalf. When power would be handed down to the next emperor, his possession of this seal left his entitlement to the crown unquestioned."

"So are you saying some Chinese emperor came here?" Reading motioned toward the armor. "And was wearing this when he met his maker?"

Acton shook his head. "Unlikely. More likely it was given by the emperor to prove they were here under his authority." Acton turned to Morales. "I assume you agree this is the Heirloom Seal of the Realm?"

"Yes."

"Any theories on how it got here?"

Morales shook his head. "I don't need theories." He pointed to several pieces of parchment lying on the platform where the seal had sat, undisturbed for centuries. "These tell us the entire story."

Acton inhaled quickly, Laura darting forward. She glanced at Morales. "What do they say?"

Morales grinned at her excitement. "It would appear that a thousand years ago, the Mayans fought a war against the Chinese."

Pacific Coastal Region
Maya Highlands, Maya Empire
1092 AD

Cheng Jun stared, wide-eyed at the old, mostly naked man yelling at them, shaking his spear. He was no threat, though the jungle was clearly thick with others, some now venturing onto the edge of the beach, leaving the protection and anonymity of the trees. Yet all wore simple garments covering little, all carrying rudimentary, primitive weapons.

They would be no match should this escalate, yet despite knowing these simple people could be easily defeated, he found his heart pounding and his hands shaking as something his father said echoed in his head.

"A single man can defeat an entire army if his heart is pure."

He was here to conquer, and this man, these men, were here to protect their land.

Whose heart is more pure?

He feared he was on the wrong side of right today. Though Admiral Khong seemed to have little doubt, simply staring at the man as if amused.

"They obviously don't want us here," muttered someone.

"That is not their choice," replied the Admiral, the soldier who had made the observation stunned he had been heard, shrinking back through the ranks. Admiral Khong beckoned his aide, and the case containing the seal was brought forward. "The holy Emperor has commanded we be here, and none have greater authority in the realm of man except the gods." Admiral Khong sneered at the old man. "And I don't see any here today."

His men chuckled, even a nervous laugh escaping Cheng's lips. Khong opened the case and removed the seal, its brilliant green shining in the fading sunlight. Cheng's eyes widened as he dropped to a knee with the others, never before having seen it, never before having seen anything so beautiful—and priceless.

Khong turned toward the old man who had fallen silent, staring at the seal still held over the Admiral's head. "You will bow before your new masters. This seal proves my authority is granted by the great Emperor Zhezong himself. And should you not heed my words, you shall die."

The old man tore his eyes away from the seal and instead shook his spear at it, resuming his shouting. As Cheng stared at him, he realized there was no anger here, only fear. This man feared them for some reason, though they had done nothing but land on their shores. He could see how that could be interpreted as a hostile act.

If he were in charge, perhaps he would have taken a seat in front of the old man and had tea and food brought out. Invite the man to a peaceful, civil act, to establish trust. After all, if they were here to establish contact, to see what riches may be found, wouldn't it be easier to have the native population show them where the gold and jewels were, rather than search for it blindly?

But he wasn't in charge, and never would be with thinking like that. The Admiral was in command, he was their leader, and Cheng had to trust that he knew best.

The Admiral drew his sword and swung, slicing the old man's stomach open, his innards spilling onto the pristine beach.

The forest went silent

Then there was a single cry.

Quintana Roo Cartel Lab #3
South of Tepich, Mexico
Present Day

Rosa Carona wiped the sweat off her brow, the heat stifling inside the lab where she worked. There was no air conditioning here, though there were large fans providing ventilation at the far end of the underground complex. Unfortunately, only one of the three was working at the moment. Her eyes were red and tearing despite the goggles she wore, and her nose, throat, and lungs burned, the thin mask she wore clearly not effective against the fumes allowed to build up due to the faulty ventilation.

Yet she kept her mouth shut.

They all did.

This wasn't some cushy factory job in the United States. This was Mexico. This was a drug lab.

And she was a criminal.

Not by choice, of course, though perhaps that was putting it rather naively. She was here, by choice, in that she had asked for and got the job, knowing what she was getting herself into. But not by choice, in that she had been so desperate for work, and this the only job available, she had been forced to take it.

Her husband was a diabetic and had recently lost his foot, no longer able to work the fields. Their children, all four of them, were under the age of eight, unable to support the family.

That left her.

They had no family here to help them, having spent all their money to move here thanks to her husband's job offer from an old friend. Things had been good for the past several years, a roof over their heads, food on their table, a little drink in the evenings. It was a small, friendly town they had found, and she was happy—they all were happy.

Until her husband became sick.

They had saved for a visit to the doctor and found out he was a diabetic. The medicine was too expensive, and after injuring his foot in the fields, it had quickly become infected, his high blood sugar preventing the healing process. Gangrene had set in after a few weeks, and the foot was amputated to save his life.

Thus ending theirs.

The same friend helped once again, giving her the name of someone to meet for work, a job only those who were desperate would take. She had refused at first, though when she dished out the last of the rice to her family, her children's bellies rumbling from hunger, her husband refusing to take his portion, instead dividing it up among the children, she had made the call.

And began making more money than she had ever dreamed possible.

There was value in keeping one's mouth shut, and that she did. She didn't make a fortune by any stretch, yet she made more than her husband ever had. Food was once again plentiful, her husband had the medicine he needed, and she had even managed to save a little with the hopes that one day they might escape this madness and move to the United States.

It was a dream, one that would probably never come true, but what was life without dreams?

Shouts from the entrance had her frozen in place, gunshots erupting followed by panicked screams. She dropped the beaker she was holding and it shattered on the floor with a hiss. Glancing over her shoulder toward the emergency exit tunnel, she grabbed her friend Louisa and ran, weaving between the long lines of tables representing millions of dollars of drugs belonging to one of the most vicious drug lords in Mexico. It didn't matter if it was the police or a rival gang, all that mattered was she couldn't be here when it was all over.

The door to the tunnel was already open, several having already entered, but the screams of terror behind her as the gunfire continued, had her realizing too few would be able to take advantage of it. She burst through the door, hauling Louisa in after her. She spun, her eyes wide as half a dozen gunmen methodically moved through the factory, killing everyone they encountered, the two guards already dead, and only a handful of women like her still alive, rushing for the exit.

She gripped the door handle, one of the gunmen spotting their escape route. He raised his machine gun and fired. She yanked the door closed, locking it like she had been taught, one of her coworkers slamming into it, hammering on the other side with her fists as she screamed for someone to open the door. Rosa reached for the lock when Louisa grabbed her arm.

"If you open it, we're all dead."

Rosa nodded, placing a hand on the door and closing her eyes. "I'm sorry."

Gunfire silenced the cries.

"Rosa, let's go!"

Louisa tugged on her shirt and Rosa reluctantly followed, sprinting down the narrow tunnel. They reached a ladder at the end, and she climbed up through a hatch that opened deep in the jungle surrounding the underground lab, the trees thick and shielding them from view. Rosa glanced about her and found only five other survivors.

Her heart sank.

There had been thirty, just like her.

"We have to get out of here before they come looking for us."

A horrific ripping sound had them all spinning toward the buried complex, a fireball erupting into the sky, black and deep orange, billowing upward and out. She gasped as the trees snapped, flattened by the explosion, tossing her off her feet. Her head hit something hard as a rush of heat and debris washed over her, and her world faded as the screams of the others died out around her.

Pacific Coastal Region
Maya Highlands, Maya Empire
1092 AD

"Father!"

Balam Canek watched in horror as his father gripped at his stomach in a futile attempt to stop the flow of blood and entrails. Balam collapsed to his knees as his father did, tears burning his eyes and rage filling his heart. His father fell to his side, the demon who had killed him so callously, glaring at the members of his tribe, holding a green talisman over his head and shouting something in defiance.

Balam pushed to his feet and looked at the others who now awaited the orders of their new chief. "Attack!"

He spun toward the demon and raised his blowgun to his mouth, loosing a tiny arrow laced with curare poison. The others followed suit, dozens of darts and spears rushing toward the murderous horde invading their land.

At first, none seemed affected, then one fell, then another. The enemy formed a circle around their leader, shields held high against the spears. A line formed behind the shields and a group of archers unleashed their arrows.

"Take cover!" Balam stepped behind a thick tree, his men doing the same, though one chose poorly, a cry of agony soon falling silent.

Balam turned to see an arrow sticking through the dead man's chest, having pierced the tree he had been hiding behind.

How is that even possible?

He poked his head out from his much larger tree and took in the battle. At least a dozen of the enemy had fallen, and they were now retreating toward the water's edge, boats pushed into the sea. His eyes fell upon the green talisman, now held under the arm of their leader. He turned to the priest. "Could that green talisman be the source of their power?"

"Absolutely."

Balam stared then made a decision, a decision that could be his last as chief. "Target their leader!"

Darts and spears rained on the group of soldiers surrounding the demon responsible for his father's death, several collapsing, the circle surrounding him spreading out to fill the gaps, leaving him more exposed. A dart made contact, the demon grasping at his neck, yanking it free and tossing it with derision to the sand as if it were nothing to be concerned with. He fell to a knee, the green talisman tumbling from his hands onto the blood-soaked sand.

Balam darted forward, racing toward the cluster of demons now concerned with their fallen leader. They dragged him toward the boat, the talisman forgotten in the sand, if only for a moment. Balam rushed past his father's body, unable to resist the urge to look upon his still form as his men rushed after him, providing him with cover. He skidded to a halt, grabbing the heavy object as the first of the enemy finally noticed him and turned to challenge him.

Balam threw his spear, puncturing the oddly thick skin, the creature's eyes bulging in shock, the fear and pain obvious, leaving him to wonder if it was but a mask covering a man's face. He grabbed his spear, yanking it from the creature's stomach, then raced back toward the trees, holding the green talisman over his head.

"I have it! I have their power!"

Universidad Veracruzana Archaeological Site
South of Tepich, Mexico
Present Day

The floor rumbled, dust from overhead shaking loose and gently falling toward them, highlighted by the battery powered lamps deployed about the chamber.

Agent Hugh Reading stared up at the ceiling. "Bloody hell, what was that?"

Professor Morales shook his head. "I don't know." He started for the stairs, Reading beating him there as everyone rushed for the open air. At first, James Acton was certain it was some type of earthquake, though having experienced those before, this felt like something different. He followed Laura out into the sunlight, several of the students outside already pointing to the horizon.

He turned and gasped, a massive dark cloud of smoke and flame rising to the north. "What's over there?"

Morales slowly shook his head. "Nothing. There shouldn't be anything there at all."

Acton's eyes narrowed. "Well, there has to be something. The jungle doesn't just explode like that."

"Whoever it is will need help," said Reading. "Can we get there by car?"

Morales vigorously shook his head. "No! We should leave it. Whatever it is, it can't be good."

"There could be people hurt!" insisted Reading. "We need to go see."

"No, there's only one thing that could be, and you don't want any part of it."

"What?"

"A drug lab."

"Or it could just be a car accident, maybe a fuel truck."

Morales sighed, conceding the point. "Yes, that is possible. But in these parts, you don't take chances."

Reading drew a deep breath, expanding his chest, his frame reaching its formidable capacity. "I'm a police officer. It's my duty to check. I'm going."

Acton stepped toward his friend. "I'll go with you. I speak Spanish."

"And I'm going with you too." Laura held out her hand. "Keys."

Morales frowned but tossed her a set. "Take mine. We're going to start packing. We can't risk being here if it's something bad. We'll head back into town when you return, just until things settle down."

"Okay, we'll be back soon."

Pacific Coastal Region
Maya Highlands, Maya Empire
1092 AD

Cheng Jun rushed to his Admiral's side, grabbing him by the arm as several of them dragged their fallen leader toward the boats. He glanced over his shoulder and spotted the imperial seal lying in the sand. "Someone get the seal!"

A man to his right turned, stepping back to retrieve the priceless jade when Cheng heard a thud and a groan. He glanced back to see the man gripping a spear in his stomach as one of the natives picked up the seal.

Admiral Khong, whose head was tilted back, gasped out a cry. "No!"

The others turned, but it was too late, the nearly naked man disappearing into the trees, the seal held over his head as he shouted something to the others, ecstatic at their victory.

For it was a victory.

They had lost this battle, lost the imperial seal, and he feared by the agony on Admiral Khong's face, they had lost their leader as well.

Captain Tai pushed through the soldiers protecting the Admiral and dropped to a knee beside him. "Admiral, are you okay?"

Khong reached up and grabbed Tai by the back of his neck, pulling him closer. "Retrieve the seal at all costs."

The words were gasped, strangled, delivered with such effort, and such conviction, there could be no denying the final order.

"You have my word, Admiral."

Khong's hand slipped from Tai's neck as he collapsed to the sand, his chest giving one final, jarring heave, then a long, stuttering sigh escaped as his last breath was exhaled on this foreign soil he had come to claim, it instead claiming him.

Cheng pointed to the trees where he had seen the native flee. "Sir, he went through there. If we go now, we can catch him!"

Captain Tai shook his head. "No, not now." He gestured toward the sun setting on the horizon. "They will have us at too great a disadvantage if we pursue them through their own territory in the dark."

"But they'll get away!"

Tai glared at him. "You question my orders?"

Cheng dropped to his knees, prostrating himself. "Forgive me, my lord, I did not mean to. I am just upset over the Admiral's death and eager to avenge him."

Tai stepped toward him, his feet stopping inches from Cheng's face. "Rise."

He did, keeping his chin tight against his chest, his eyes focused on the ground. "You will have your chance, tomorrow." Tai turned to the others. "These primitives were here when we arrived, which means they live nearby. They will no doubt return to their homes, drunk with the mistaken belief that they have won. They will feast and celebrate, and tomorrow, when their stomachs are overburdened and their heads are swollen from drink, we will attack."

Cheng smiled, the wisdom of their new commander evident, the other men around them murmuring their agreement.

"Bring everyone ashore except skeleton crews for each ship. Bring every weapon we have and all the supplies. We won't be leaving until we have retrieved the imperial seal, and punished those responsible for the Admiral's death!"

Cheng stared at the now silent forest, their attackers having disappeared with the seal. Though he agreed with his new commander's orders to attack in the morning, he wondered how they would beat what had appeared to be an inferior enemy, yet clearly wasn't. He looked about at the dead and dying, some felled by spears, but others with no wounds evident, their bodies contorted as if frozen in place, their eyes staring into nothingness as if their souls still remained, confused about what had just happened.

How had they died?

How had they been killed?

He spotted something sticking in the arm of one of his fallen comrades, a tiny piece of wood with what appeared to be feathers surrounding it. He took a knee and pulled it free, a small bead of blood left behind. He examined the tiny creation, his eyes narrowing.

It's a dart!

But how could something so small kill? He searched about and found dozens of the darts littering the sand. He picked one up and placed it on his tongue. A harsh, bitter taste caused him to spit onto the sand the saliva that had quickly formed. "Sir, these darts, they're poison!"

Captain Tai spun toward him. "Show me."

Cheng held it out and Tai reached for it. "Careful, sir. One prick could kill you."

Tai paused, his arm recoiling quickly. He leaned in, examining the tiny device then turned to the men. "Full armor tomorrow, with thick clothing underneath. We must defend against these"—he paused, turning back to stare at the dart still held in Cheng's hand—"things. In the morning, their greatest weapon will be no danger. Tomorrow, we will have our revenge!"

Quintana Roo Cartel Compound
Tepich, Mexico
Present Day

Javier Diaz sauntered onto the marble patio surrounding the large infinity pool, his boss, known to everyone only as El Jefe, sat in the hot tub, a buxom American blonde on either arm, the boss' wife visiting her family in Guadalajara.

While the cat's away…

"El Jefe, there's something you need to see out front."

El Jefe frowned, clearly not pleased at the disturbance. A third woman appeared from under the water, one of her friends swapping positions.

Oh, to be king! One of these days.

"What is it?" He was annoyed, and annoying El Jefe was never wise.

"I'm sorry to disturb you, El Jefe, but there's a delivery for you from Galano." The mention of El Jefe's rival changed the mood and he reached under the water, swatting the girl away as he rose. Diaz turned so he wouldn't have the image of his rotund boss' pito burned onto his retinas.

El Jefe stepped from the pool, one of the many servants wrapping him in a robe. "A delivery? From that puta? What is it?"

Diaz brightened slightly. "A car!"

El Jefe's eyes narrowed. "A car?" He strode through the patio doors and into the living room twice as large as Diaz's entire home. "Did you check it over?"

"Yes, sir, bumper to bumper. It's clean. And very nice."

El Jefe glanced at him, as if dismissing his underling's opinion as unworthy of consideration. They emerged through the front doors, the gleaming metallic silver of a Jag convertible greeting him, Galano's right-hand man, Sanchez, sitting on the hood, a cigar chomped between his teeth. He rose, presenting the car with a sweep of his hand and a bow.

"El Jefe, a gift from Señor Galano. An apology, if you will, for last week's incident."

Diaz frowned, stepping slightly away from El Jefe. Last week, three of their men had been gunned down by Galano's men in a bar brawl in town. Overtures had been immediately made, Galano sending the men responsible over, El Jefe executing them personally.

There was an uneasy truce in the area, most of the money to be made not from the local trade, but from exporting to the United States. And the market there was so massive, there was plenty of room for more than one operator. As long as they kept out of each other's way.

And tequila and whores too often led to disputes, like last week.

"He would like you to have his prize Jag as an expression of his sorrow at your loss."

El Jefe walked around the car, nodding slowly, clearly appreciating the sleek lines of what Diaz was convinced was the most beautiful car he had ever seen in person.

"It's like a James Bond car, El Jefe!" He grinned at the others as heads bobbed in agreement.

El Jefe grunted then walked over to one of the guards, holding his hand out. "Gun." An AR-15 rifle was handed over and El Jefe spun toward the car, emptying the magazine into it, starting from the hood and working his way back. The weapon spent, he tossed it back at the shocked guard as Sanchez backed away, his hands on his head.

"What did you do that for? You realize how expensive that is? You realize that this was a gift?"

El Jefe raised a finger, silencing everyone. "No, this was an insult. You and I both know this piece of shit breaks down all the time on him. He only wanted to unload his problem on me!" He pointed at Sanchez. "Now get your ass out of here before I have my men pump you full of lead." He started toward the door then stopped. "And take this junk with you."

One of the minions rushed up to Diaz, holding out a tablet. "Javier. From Lab Three, just south of here."

Diaz watched the video showing a dozen armed men entering their lab to the south, those inside slaughtered before the video abruptly cut off. "What happened?"

"We think the lab exploded. There were ventilation problems. Probably a spark ignited the whole thing."

"Okay." He sucked in a deep breath, hating to be the one to deliver more bad news to El Jefe. "El Jefe, we've got a problem."

El Jefe continued through the living room and back to the hot tub, apparently determined to resume his extra-marital activities. "What is it?"

"It looks like Lab Three was hit. And exploded."

This brought the man to a halt. Diaz showed him the video. El Jefe sighed deeply, clearly battling the rage building within. "Survivors?"

Diaz tapped a few icons, another display appearing. "Looks like we've got a few."

El Jefe lowered into the hot tub. "Okay, check it out. Clean up the mess."

"By clean up…"

"Kill any survivors, dump the bodies near town. I don't want anything tracing back to us."

"Yes, sir."

A blonde dipped under the water. "Oh, and when you're done, take the boys out. Show them a good time. I don't want to see you back before tomorrow."

Diaz grinned. "Yes, sir!"

Pacific Coastal Region
Maya Highlands, Maya Empire
1092 AD

Balam Canek glanced over at Nelli, standing at the edge of the crowd, her arms folded, her eyes downcast. She stole a glance at him, catching his eyes, and they both exchanged a slight smile he hoped would be missed by those gathered. They had lost several good men in the battle, but the enemy had suffered a great defeat. He held the green talisman high, tilted his head back, and roared at the gods. The thunderous response from the villagers echoed in his chest, and as he returned his gaze to them, he caught a glimpse of the now empty refugee camp, his father's last orders fulfilled while they had been in battle.

His chest ached for the loss of his friend, Kawil, but there had been no choice. Clearly the gods were angry, having dispatched an army of demons to their shores, though the fact they had been allowed to win the battle suggested there was mercy in the hearts of their gods, his father's actions of expelling those who had broken the faith, perhaps the act of contrition the gods needed to forgive them.

Yet the battle wasn't over.

As if sensing his thoughts, one of the lookouts left at the beach sprinted from the trees, racing toward him.

"Sir, I have word from the beach." The runner rested his hands on his knees as he hunched over, gasping for air.

"What is it?"

"They haven't left the beach, but more are arriving and supplies are coming from the belly of the floating…" He paused, confused. "I'm sorry, Chief, but I don't know what to call them. They float like a boat, but are as big as an island."

They float like a boat…

And then it made sense. It wasn't floating islands or giant sea creatures he had been seeing, but boats. Boats bigger than any he could have possibly imagined before today.

These demons are truly powerful!

"How will we defeat them, Chief? We are but a few!"

Those gathered repeated the question in murmurs, fear and doubt gripping them all.

And they were right.

They were lucky. They had surprised the enemy, the servants of the gods clearly not expecting to be challenged by mere mortals. And they wouldn't be so easily defeated next time, not by such a small group.

He turned to a throng of young boys, too young to fight effectively. "Go to the surrounding villages, tell them what has happened, and have them send all their warriors to fight. Tell them they must be here by daybreak, or all could be lost."

The boys exchanged glances, the names of nearby villages whispered among them as they divvied up the responsibilities, then they were gone.

He turned to those who remained. "We may have won this battle, but they will be coming for this tomorrow." He held up the talisman.

"But Chief, shouldn't we give it back to them? Perhaps then they will leave us alone?"

Murmurs of assent washed through his subjects.

"They killed my father, our chief, though he had not harmed them with anything but words. They are on our shores uninvited, displaying nothing but their evil visage and their weapons. They did not come here as friends, but as enemies, and nothing that has happened here today, will change that. They will come for us, even if we return their talisman. We must be ready for them, and we must defeat them, or we all shall die."

"But how?"

Balam jabbed a finger at the ground. "This is our home." He pointed at the trees. "This is our forest. We know this land like the back of our hands, and we will use this knowledge to fight them. Off the open beach and among the trees we grew up in, they will lose their numerical advantage. And once the others arrive to help us, these demons will lose. We know they can be killed, therefore we know they are not gods. They may have been sent by the gods, but they are *not* gods! We will prevail, and when we do, exact our revenge for the death of my father! The forest will run red with their blood!"

South of Tepich, Mexico
Present Day

"There!"

Laura pointed from between the seats, Acton cranking the wheel to the left, propelling them down a nearly invisible road cut into the jungle. The smoke had mostly cleared, the intensity of whatever blast that had occurred, evidently burning itself out quickly. That fact, and the fact they were now off the road, thus likely eliminating a car accident as the cause, had her nervous, Morales' warning of a possible drug lab now more plausible.

Acton slammed the brakes on, bringing them to a skidding halt. The devastation was shocking. The trees were all knocked down around them, flattened like she had seen in footage of nuclear testing, though only for about fifty feet from what appeared to be a crater, whatever had once been there now nothing but smoking ruins. Bodies were strewn about, some burnt horribly, others mangled messes, tossed about like the Devil's playthings.

"What the bloody hell happened here?" They climbed out, Laura walking to the edge of the crater and staring down into the pit, cinder block walls mostly still in place, the shattered remains of tables and other equipment strewn about, charred bodies blasted to the outer walls.

"I think Eduardo was right. This was probably a drug lab." Acton pointed at some of the bodies. "These guys all have guns. Guards, maybe?"

Reading grunted. "Or a rival gang hit the place. The chemicals involved in these labs are highly volatile. If a stray bullet hit the wrong thing…" He paused and frowned. "Boom."

Laura stepped back, unable to look anymore. "I don't think anyone survived this."

A sound from the woods had her rethinking her last statement. She beckoned to the others and they headed for the edge of the jungle where the trees were still standing. She pushed aside some branches and stopped, half a dozen women huddled together, whimpering, tears streaking their faces, faces showing evidence of minor wounds probably received in the blast. They cried out and backed away as Reading appeared beside her. Laura held out a hand, stopping him, then approached the women.

"It's okay, you're safe now."

Pacific Coastal Region
Maya Highlands, Maya Empire
1092 AD

Cheng Jun advanced several paces then raised a hand, the men behind him stopping as he listened for any sign of the enemy.

Nothing.

And it had been that way for the past hour, their slow advance through the thick forest hampered not only by the dense undergrowth, but their fear of walking into a hail of poison darts.

"Look!" hissed one of the men, and Cheng turned to see where he was pointing. He could see nothing at first, then as his eyes adjusted, he saw the distinct outline of a head and shoulder sticking out from behind a large tree. The shadow disappeared.

"We're being watched."

Captain Tai came up from behind, adorned in the armor of the Admiral, a distasteful act in Cheng's opinion. Nothing but Tai's eyes were revealed by the helmet he now wore, and Cheng had to admit he appeared intimidating. Cheng adjusted his own mask, most of the soldiers now wearing anything that would cover exposed skin from the deadly darts their enemy seemed so adept at firing. And it made for an uncomfortable foray. He was already drenched in sweat, as were the others, the forest hot and damp, the several layers of clothing soaked through and clinging to his skin. Though he'd rather bake than die in agony from the tiniest of pricks.

"Pursue!"

Cheng jumped forward, the order foolish, though not to be disobeyed. He could hear the footfalls of his comrades as it seemed every stick on the forest floor was trampled, their approach anything but stealthy. Yet he understood the thinking. Capture this one man, and he could lead them to where their enemy was hiding.

Someone cried out to his left and he glanced over his shoulder, seeing nothing out of the ordinary, when his right foot gave way, someone beside him disappearing from sight. He reached out with his left hand and grabbed the arm of another as he struggled to regain his balance, his eyes staring in horror at the pit that had opened beside him, sharpened sticks embedded in the bottom, now impaling one of his comrades.

"Careful, they've laid traps for us!" he cried, and the mad rush quickly slowed, someone else screaming to his right.

"Halt!" ordered Captain Tai, and they all froze. "Shields!"

Balam Canek motioned silently to the others and raised his blowgun to his lips, those to his left and right doing the same. He stepped out from behind the sturdy tree shielding him and took aim. He inhaled then placed his mouth over the pipe, rapidly exhaling, sending the poisoned dart spiraling toward these demon spawn, his heart pounding at the sight of their leader, still adorned in gold, alive once again.

It was disheartening to know he couldn't be killed, at least not with the poison. Yet should they eliminate his guard, and bring him down once again, fire would be the order of the day.

But first, they had to win.

Hundreds of darts flew silently through the air, and several of their enemy collapsed, though not as many as he had hoped. Today, they appeared to be wearing thick hides and masks, no doubt to protect themselves from the poison. He fired again, reaching down and pulling another from his belt, careful not to poke himself.

No more dropped, this tactic clearly failing.

He motioned over his head to fall back, and they quietly retreated into the darkness, leaving their enemy frozen, wondering if the attack would continue.

And with each delay, it bought them time, time for the warriors of the surrounding villages to arrive.

Universidad Veracruzana Archaeological Site
South of Tepich, Mexico
Present Day

"You stay with them, keep them calm. I'll go tell Eduardo that we're back."

Acton nodded as Laura headed for the discovery site, he and Reading already tending to the minor wounds suffered by the women the moment they had come to a halt. The ride back had been tight, the six women nearly stacked in the back seat of the SUV, Reading doing the driving while she sat in her husband's lap. She pushed through the thick jungle, following the trampled path to the discovery site, and emerged from the trees.

Morales rushed toward her. "Thank God you're okay!"

Laura waved. "You were right. It was a drug lab. Completely destroyed."

Morales' eyes widened as his face paled slightly. He turned to the students, saying something in Spanish that resulted in an increased flurry of activity.

"We found six survivors."

Everyone froze, turning to stare at her.

"Ahh, what did you do with them?"

Laura's eyebrows popped. "Well, we couldn't exactly leave them there."

"Please tell me they're not here."

"Well, of course they are. Like I said, we couldn't leave them there, so we took them with us. We'll take them into town."

"Oh no, oh no, oh no." Morales paced in a circle, pulling on his beard, working himself into a panic. "Why did you do that? Why did you bring them here?" he muttered, clearly not expecting an answer. He froze then spun toward her. "We have to get out of here, now."

His demeanor now had her on edge as well. The students were clearly scared, and Morales was terrified. They knew their country and this area better than she did, suggesting perhaps his panic was justified.

Maybe bringing them with us was a bad idea.

There had been the option of simply calling for help, yet at the time, it had seemed wise to take these frightened women away from the danger. And it had been the right move. No one could convince her that they had been wrong. These women appeared innocent to her, clearly in need of help, and no threat to anyone.

"Let's go, now!"

The students grabbed their already packed bags, and a line quickly formed, pushing through the jungle, toward the waiting vehicles. Laura hung back, bringing up the rear with Morales. They arrived in the cleared area, the rear of the pickup truck already filled with the survivors, Reading and Acton waiting for them. The students piled into the second vehicle, quickly filling it to capacity, four more squeezing into the cab of the pickup.

"There's not enough room!" cried Morales, pulling again at his beard.

"They can come back for us." Laura handed one of the students her satphone. "Keep this with you in case something goes wrong. When you get to town, send the police back to get us."

"Okay, señora."

Laura stepped back, the engine roaring to life, when the survivors all cried out, reaching for her, an explosion of words erupting. "What's wrong?" she asked, looking at Morales then Acton.

"Looks like they want you to come with them."

"I guess you've made quite the impression on them." Acton stepped closer. "Go with them. There's room."

"But I want to stay with you."

He shook his head. "And I want you out of here. We don't know what's going on. The sooner you're safe in town, the sooner I'll breathe easy."

She frowned, but nodded. "Fine. I'll call Greg when I get there and let him know what's going on. And the embassy, just in case."

Acton smiled. "Good thinking." He gave her a kiss. "Love you."

"Love you too." She reached up and was pulled into the back of the truck, the women squeezing together tightly to make room for her, smiles all around as their savior was now with them. The two trucks peeled away in a cloud of dust, Laura unable to see her beloved, praying he would be safe, and she would see him again, very soon.

Quintana Roo Cartel Lab #3
South of Tepich, Mexico

Javier Diaz stood with his hands on his hips, staring at the open pit that only hours ago had been one of their most profitable labs, producing over five million dollars' worth of fentanyl a month. But no matter. They would build another one, and production would be back to normal within two weeks.

This was what the government couldn't understand. They could take down the drug labs, but unless they removed the demand, there would always be incentive, and massive profits, to rebuild, and rebuild quickly. If he knew El Jefe, he'd rebuild even bigger so he could produce even more. This would be a minor hiccup, there still another dozen labs hidden throughout the region, still producing.

"Hey, Javier, take a look at this. I recognize him."

Diaz walked over to one of the bodies impaled on a branch nearby. His eyes narrowed. "Isn't that Carlos, one of Galano's men?"

"Yup."

"That sonofabitch. The balls on him! To give a gift to El Jefe while hitting one of our labs? Unbelievable!"

"I guess El Jefe was right. It was an insult, after all."

Diaz pulled out his satphone. "El Jefe will want to know right away."

"War?"

"Oh yeah, this means war all right." He pressed the button to make a call, but the display flashed then went dead. "Shit." He tossed it toward one of his men. "It's dead. The charger is in the glove compartment." His man caught it then climbed into the vehicle. Diaz slowly turned, examining the scene. "Okay, there's no way for this to be traced back to us except through people. Let's gather up our guys—"

"Hey, Javier, looks like we've got survivors."

Diaz spun toward one of his men, waving a tracker.

"Southeast of here, heading this way fast."

Diaz twirled his hand over his head, signaling his men to get in the SUVs. "Let's clean this mess up."

En route to Tepich, Mexico

Laura tightly gripped the tailgate of the pickup truck, wedged into the corner by the other women, there barely room for the seven of them. Despite the fact they would be in town shortly, none of these women seemed happy or even relieved. Fear still dominated their faces, their eyes wide as they stared at the road ahead, as if worried something might yet come to claim their lives.

The woman beside her, who she had learned was named Rosa and who spoke excellent English, clung to her arm like a child. She was perhaps twenty-five, the women a mix of ages and sizes, the drug lords apparently not choosing their female workers based upon their potential sex appeal.

Which made sense. The last thing a drug lord would need is having his men too busy keeping their eyes on asses rather than assets. She felt sorry for them. How bad did things have to be to knowingly work in a drug lab, to work for criminals, surrounded by dangerous chemicals all day?

She was obscenely wealthy thanks to her late brother who had left her hundreds of millions after he died, money he had earned selling his hi-tech company years before. She and Acton didn't live an ostentatious lifestyle except when they traveled, private jets their preferred mode of transportation. They still lived in Acton's home, bought on a professor's salary, drove regular cars, and rarely ate at expensive restaurants. They were down to earth people who enjoyed the basics.

Good home cooked meals with a nice glass of wine, a snifter of scotch, or a bottle of beer—whatever was appropriate to the occasion. She didn't consider themselves snobs, and would be horrified if she found out anyone did think of them that way.

They were generous, though usually through anonymous gestures, though now most students knew who was funding their trips when they couldn't afford them. All they insisted upon was hard work and dedication from their students, no matter who was footing the bill. And if their extra money meant solar panels and air conditioning in the tents in Egypt, then so be it.

A luxury shared.

And the occasional plane ticket for a friend who couldn't afford it, just made her feel good. She thought of Reading, waiting back at the archaeological site with her husband and Morales, and closed her eyes, picturing the first time she had seen him at her old haunt, the British Museum. She had met Acton for the first time just that day, yanked into a maelstrom of danger and confusion resulting in her arrest by the very man she now considered one of her closest friends, all over a crystal skull she had dedicated her life to studying. Her life had changed so much over the past few years, it was breathtaking at times.

She was now married to an incredible man, lived and worked in the United States, and led a life that never wanted to give them a moment of peace. She loved the adventure, the intrigue, the taste of discovery, though could do without the guns and explosions and cults and terrorists.

She sighed, her heart slamming as she tried to ignore the insanity of the student driver as he raced full-tilt on the gravel road, following the other vehicle ahead of them in a desperate attempt to reach town before something went wrong.

We're more likely to end up wrecked than accosted by some drug gang.

Red lights shone brightly ahead of them, and they were all tossed forward as their driver applied the brakes, both vehicles skidding to a halt. Laura pushed to her feet and peered through the dust, her heart skipping a beat at the sight of two black SUVs, blocking the road ahead, at least half a dozen men emerging, guns drawn. She slammed on the roof of the truck with her fist.

"Get us out of here!" The ignition cranked, the old truck having stalled out, probably from a two-footed braking maneuver and a forgotten clutch. Gunfire erupted, the lead truck's windows shattered, the students inside screaming. "Everybody out!" cried Laura, leaping over the side and onto the gravel road. She reached in and pulled the woman who had been holding her arm to the ground, the others following.

She raced for the trees only feet away, plunging into the thick cover as the gunmen turned their attention on the stalled truck. She glanced over her shoulder and cried out as she watched the three students crammed in the front shake from the impacts of the bullets, the women surrounding the truck, some running down the road, away from the shooters, mowed down as the onslaught continued, unabated.

She looked about her and found only Rosa had made it. She grabbed her hand and they rushed deeper into the jungle, putting as much distance as they could between them and the shooters.

Then there was silence.

She froze, pulling Rosa to a halt and slapping a hand over the woman's mouth. She continued slowly forward, pulling them deeper into the woods, carefully watching her footing, avoiding any dried branches strewn along the jungle floor, all the while listening for any signs of pursuit.

There were none.

They must not have seen us.

Doors slammed shut and engines roared to life, the sounds of departing vehicles filling the air, then nothing.

"Stay here," she whispered, but the woman shook her head vigorously, latching onto Laura's arm. "Okay, but be quiet. Watch your step." The woman nodded then followed her, gripping Laura's hand as she led them back to the roadway. She pushed through the trees and gasped.

All four vehicles were gone, as were the bodies. All that remained were shell casings and blood. And two billowing clouds of dust in either direction. Her eyes bulged as she realized one of those clouds was headed toward the discovery site.

James!

She yanked her hand free and sprinted after them.

Pacific Coastal Region
Maya Highlands, Maya Empire
1092 AD

Cheng Jun picked his way carefully through the trees, leading what had been twenty men along their left flank in an attempt to outmaneuver the enemy. While the main body of their force continued noisily forward, two groups had been dispatched on their flanks, small enough to move forward quickly and quietly with the hopes they could come in from behind and trap their enemy between two fronts.

And it was working.

Somewhat.

Their force of twenty had dwindled to a mere dozen, traps and one-off surprise attacks by lone defenders having pared down their numbers, though each time they had also drawn blood, preserving the balance, and the secrecy of their presence.

He heard something to his right and held up his hand, everyone stopping. He peered through the trees and smiled. There were dozens of the enemy, hiding in the trees, all facing the approaching main body—their backs to him and his men. He pointed so everyone could see where the enemy lay, then positioned himself behind a large tree, waiting for Captain Tai to arrive.

He regarded the dozen men with him, wondering if it would be enough. It would be should the second group flanking to the right had successfully arrived as well, though all they had to do was sow confusion among the enemy's ranks. It would give Tai's group enough time to reach them, then they would all make quick work of this inferior force.

Branches snapped nearby and he dropped low as a young boy sprinted through the trees, oblivious to the danger lurking nearby. He reached the group of enemy soldiers, excitedly exchanging words with what must be their leader. The leader appeared unhappy with the report, exchanging glances with the others, one of them running away, a second following. Harsh words were snapped and the rest of the line held, though it was evident discontent had infested the ranks.

This could work to our advantage.

Balam Canek buried his anger. The runner had just informed him that no warriors from the surrounding villages would be joining them in the battle, all apparently too scared to engage an army sent by the gods. He was certain if he had gone himself to solicit support, he would have succeeded, the young boys sent commanding no respect from the other chiefs. Yet that hadn't been an option.

His place was with his people in this time of crisis.

As he eyed the approaching enemy, numbering at least a hundred men, he regarded his paltry force of less than fifty, now short two more who had panicked. They had eliminated perhaps half of the enemy through their traps and ambushes, lost at least a dozen of their own, and he now no longer had confidence they would win the day, their delaying tactics for naught. This would be a war of attrition, whittling down their enemy one by one then fleeing before they could regroup.

There would be no single, great engagement with hundreds of fierce Mayan warriors battling the minions of the gods.

He looked at the others. "Do not lose faith, my brothers, for I believe the gods are on our side today." He raised his hands to his mouth and executed a birdcall, echoed several times in return, then readied himself as several of the others removed their tinder bundles, blowing gently on them until they smoked then finally burst into flame. The moment the flames appeared, casting a bright glow on their surroundings, he heard the others, concealed high in the trees above the enemy, execute their deadly task.

Universidad Veracruzana Archaeological Site
South of Tepich, Mexico
Present Day

Javier Diaz stepped out of the SUV and glanced around, not bothering to draw his weapon. It was quiet. Too quiet. He examined the muddy clearing, there no doubt vehicles had been here recently. He turned to one of his men. "You're sure this is where they came from?"

The tracker was waved at him. "According to this, they came here for a few minutes, then left."

"Hey, Javier, there's a trail over here. Looks like fresh footprints."

Diaz walked over and took a look, there no doubt a significant number of people had been through here, probably the people with the missing workers. "Let's go." He pushed through the trees, following the trail for several minutes before emerging in a clearing, a curious scene laid out in front of him, a grid work of stakes and twine covering a large area surrounding a stone archway. He knew enough to know it was probably Mayan, their ruins all over this part of the country, though hadn't been aware something was so close to their operation.

"Looks like some sort of Indiana Jones shit going on here, hey?"

"Yeah. This looks new. It's going to draw attention to the area. El Jefe will want to know." He walked over to the archway and peered inside, a set of stone stairs leading down. He heard voices and held up his fist, silencing the others. He drew his weapon and began down the stairs, gesturing for his men to follow.

"Do you think it will be safe if we just leave it?"

Professor Morales shrugged at Acton's question. "Sure. It has been for a thousand years, what's another few days?"

Acton's eyebrows rose. "A thousand? You mentioned that before. Don't you mean five hundred?"

Morales shook his head. "No, this is pre-Columbian." He pointed at some hieroglyphs on a nearby wall. "According to this, it was built shortly after the arrival of our Chinese friend here, and according to the Mayan calendar here, that would put it around 1092 AD."

Reading's eyebrows rose. "That's rather precise, isn't it?"

"Yes, absolutely. The Mayans were extremely accurate with their calendars, their entire civilization was built around understanding the positions of the sun, moon, planets, even the stars. Their pyramids were built with the positioning in mind, and they were able to use their knowledge to predict eclipses, and by doing so, the priests were able to trick the people into thinking their prayers and sacrifices were having an effect, by timing rituals around these events."

"Sounds pretty sketchy."

Morales smiled. "It was. But the Mayans lasted for thousands of years, and probably would have lasted much longer if it weren't for the arrival of my ancestors."

Acton agreed. "True, though the droughts by the time Columbus had arrived had pretty much done them in."

"They still might have recovered." Morales held out his hands, shaking them at the room. "Look at this! We're going to learn so much!"

Acton smiled at his friend. "And you're sure we can leave it unattended?"

"Absolutely. Nobody knows we're here except for my students, and they should be arriving in town shortly. When we're picked up, I'll arrange for the university to have security sent before we return."

Acton frowned. "And whoever owned that drug lab won't come snooping around?"

Morales shrugged. "Why would they? The lab is kilometers from here, and I doubt those women even knew where you took them. Besides, they never saw anything but where we parked. In a few days, this will all be over."

Footsteps echoing down the stairs had them all freeze, Reading backing away and put himself between whoever was about to arrive and the other two men.

Acton leaned to the side, peering around Reading's broad shoulders. "Umm, Laura, is that you?"

The steps continued, several distinct sets now clearly heard. Acton's eyes darted around the room, searching for a weapon, finding nothing he'd be willing to risk damaging merely to save his life. Four men emerged, the first spraying the ceiling with a burst of gunfire as the others spread out, weapons aimed at them.

"Are there more?" asked the apparent leader in Spanish.

Morales shook his head. "Just us."

The answer wasn't believed, a wave of the gun sending two of the men to search the other chambers before returning.

"Nobody else, Javier."

The leader raised his weapon. "Sorry about this. It's just business."

Acton decided to take a chance and appeal for their lives in the only way he could think of. He stepped forward, past Reading, his hands up. "Wait! I'm American, and I'm rich."

Better include the others.

"We all are. We'll pay you whatever you want."

This had the desired effect of giving the man pause. He lowered his weapon slightly. "Okay, don't kill the gringo, kill the others."

The weapons rose again and Acton stepped forward some more, and in perfect Spanish, said, "Kill anyone, and you'll get nothing."

Javier Diaz eyed the gringo, frowning. If it were true, and this man was rich—these *men* were rich—then there might be a hefty ransom to be had. He sneered at the obvious Mexican. "You're not rich."

The man's eyes cast to the floor and the gringo stepped in front of him.

"He's rich because he's with me. Anything happens to my friends, anything at all, and you get nothing. Let us go, and I promise you we'll pay whatever you want."

Diaz's eyes narrowed. "Say I wanted ten million dollars?"

"Then you'd have it."

Diaz's mouth went slightly dry. "Each."

The gringo frowned. "Now you're just being greedy."

"Each."

The man sighed. "Fine. But nobody gets hurt."

Diaz smiled. "I'll take you to El Jefe. He'll decide if you're worth the trouble."

"Who's El Jefe?"

Diaz noticed the Mexican go pale. He gestured toward him with his gun. "Ask him. He knows."

The gringo turned. "Who's El Jefe?"

"One of the most vicious drug dealers in all of Mexico."

Universidad Veracruzana Archaeological Site
South of Tepich, Mexico

Laura stopped running, pressing her hand against her side, the stitch now unbearable. She gasped in lungful after lungful of air, swearing to get more cardio in when this was all over. She had let her fitness lag since being shot in the stomach, and though she now felt she was fully recovered, she had only recovered to the point someone living her lifestyle could.

Too many private jets and luxuries on the digs.

She glanced back to see Rosa in the distance, clearly out of shape compared to her. Laura left the road, following the rough trail cut into the jungle by the students so they could fit their trucks through, the parking area only a few hundred feet from here. She made her way quickly and quietly, not sure of what she might find, still hoping whoever had gone in this direction had driven right past, the only way they could possibly know of this place would be if someone had survived and told them. Part of her hoped there had been more, though another part hoped there hadn't been, selfishly placing more value on the lives of the ones she knew and loved, than the strangers she had only met today. It made her feel guilty.

Slightly.

She froze, spotting the glint of something through the leaves. She ducked into the trees and rounded the clearing, the two black SUVs from earlier parked in the center, one man leaning on the hood, smoking a cigarette, his back to her. She looked about but saw no one else.

They must be at the site.

If they were, then Acton and the others could already be dead. Yet kidnapping was big business in Mexico, and a rich American could prove valuable. If Acton had been given time to negotiate with them, then he would have played the money card.

And greed had a way of making people do stupid things.

Like keep people alive you shouldn't.

She reached for her satphone then cursed, remembering she had given it to one of the students. And it forced a decision. If they were dead, then what she did now meant nothing. Though if they were alive, and were to be taken hostage, she had to delay things. She searched around her feet and spotted a fist-sized stone. She picked it up and quietly stepped into the clearing, striding swiftly and surely toward the man as he flicked his spent cigarette into the mud. She swung, smacking his head hard. He collapsed in a heap, never having seen his attacker.

She pulled a knife from his belt and ran around both vehicles, slicing all of the tires while keeping a wary eye on the path leading to the library. As she stabbed the last tire, she rose, her eye spotting something sitting on the dash.

A satphone.

She opened the door and reached in, yanking it free of its charger. She rushed back toward the woods as Rosa arrived, gasping for breath.

She opened her mouth to say something when Laura pressed a finger against her lips then grabbed Rosa by the arm, pulling her toward the trees as voices sounded behind her.

"What the hell is this!" Javier Diaz stood, staring agape at the flattened tires of their vehicles. "Where the hell is Ybanez?"

"Over here."

He stepped around the front of the lead vehicle to find Ybanez sitting in the mud, rubbing the back of his head. "What the hell happened?"

"Dunno. Something hit me in the back of the head. I must have blacked out."

Diaz kicked him in the side. "Not *something* you idiot, *someone*. Look at the tires!" He drew his weapon and emptied the mag into the trees, roaring with rage. He spun on his hostages. "You said you were alone!"

The gringo replied. "We are. We sent everyone to town in our only two trucks. We're just waiting for help to arrive."

Diaz glared at him then grunted. "You'll be waiting a long time." The others chuckled and he flicked a wrist across his throat, cutting them off. "Get me the phone. I'll call for someone to pick us up."

Ybanez, now on his feet, opened the door of the SUV and cursed. "It's gone!"

"What?" Diaz joined him, Ybanez pointing at the charging cable, still plugged into the cigarette lighter.

"It's gone. I left it on the dash to charge."

Diaz tilted his head back again and bellowed, birds cawing in protest, leaving their peaceful perches at the disturbance. He grabbed an AK-47 from his nearest man and sprayed the jungle until it was spent, then hurled it back at its owner. "Come out of there, or I kill your friends!"

The gringo raised a finger. "Just a reminder, they're no friend of ours. All our friends left almost an hour ago. Whoever is doing this has nothing to do with us." Diaz glared at him, but the gringo wouldn't shut up. "Perhaps it was whoever blew up your lab?"

Diaz paused, resisting the urge to pistol-whip the arrogant American. The man was right, and it wasn't something he had thought of. It wouldn't make sense for there to be someone out here alone, especially someone who would have the cojones to knock out one of his men, flatten the tires, and steal their only means of communicating with the outside world. These were just scared teachers, or archaeologists, or something.

It had to be one of Galano's men.

Or more than one.

He eyed the surrounding jungle, suddenly very aware of how alone they were. "We can't stay here." He jerked a thumb over his shoulder at the hostages. "Someone might come looking for them."

"We could walk to town."

Diaz shook his head. "No, the wrong person is liable to come by. Police or Galano's men."

Ybanez, still nursing his head, pointed to the north. "If we cut through the jungle, we can probably reach El Jefe's by end of day tomorrow." Groans from the others caused Ybanez's cheeks to burn. "Hey, just an idea."

Diaz nodded. "And our only choice. It'll keep us out of sight, and get us to where we're going eventually."

"Won't El Jefe send someone to look for us if we're not back soon?"

Diaz shook his head. "No, he told me to take you guys out on the town tonight to blow off some steam. Nobody is looking for us until tomorrow afternoon at the earliest, and we've got to warn El Jefe about Galano's attack on the lab. We're at war, and he doesn't even know it."

Laura slapped a hand over her mouth, resisting the urge to scream her terror and rage. Instead, she cringed as her husband was pistol-whipped from behind, the man she loved more than anything in the world collapsing in a heap on the ground.

"Why the bloody hell did you do that?" bellowed Reading, his hands tied behind his back as her husband's, as they were herded away from the disabled vehicles and into the jungle.

Her Spanish was limited—very limited—and she was dying to ask Rosa what had been said among the furious men now holding her husband and friends hostage. The fact they were alive, suggested Acton had convinced them they were worth more alive than dead, which meant a ransom payment was in her future. She didn't mind that, she had the money. What concerned her was that too many people in this country were taken hostage, the ransom paid, then the bodies discovered days later.

She'd cross that bridge when she came to it.

For now, they were alive and on foot, apparently their only means of communication now in her possession, and her foe concerned enough about something that waiting for help wasn't an option.

When the last of them disappeared, she waited until she could no longer hear them crashing through the jungle, then emerged from the trees. She signaled for Rosa to remain quiet, then headed back to the archaeological site. She debated going inside to check on the priceless artifacts, but decided against it.

There was no time.

She scanned the camp for supplies, spotting two backpacks nearby. She grabbed them and emptied the contents onto the ground, repacking them with two sleeping bags, a tarp, a first aid kit, a fire starting kit, half a dozen bottles of water, and some tins of food left at the camp's makeshift kitchen.

And a large hunting knife in its sheath.

Satisfied she had everything salvageable she might need, she handed a backpack to Rosa, who had stood silently, watching her with what appeared to be a combination of awe and curiosity. "Take this. It's not very heavy." Rosa nodded, shrugging her shoulders into the straps. Laura tightened them so they wouldn't chafe, then donned her own. "Now, tell me what they were saying. What's going on?"

Rosa looked toward the path leading to the parking area. "They're mad, and I think scared. They think Galano's men might be coming here, or police, so they decided to walk through the jungle and not on the road. They think they can get to El Jefe's house by tomorrow night."

Laura checked her watch. It was already early evening, the sun low on the horizon, there not much time left to travel safely. If she could get a message to the right people, help could potentially be here before tomorrow night, especially with the people she had access to.

But help could be here in minutes if she just called the local police.

"Do you know the number for the police in town?"

Rosa's eyes bulged and she waved her hands in front of her, shaking her head. "No! You can't trust them. They mostly work for El Jefe. They'll just kill us."

Laura's heart slammed as her stomach tightened. They were friends with several Delta Force members, though not close enough for her to have a phone number that could just be called. Her only choice was Acton's former student. She pulled out her cellphone, thankful it was still working, and pulled up the contacts list.

Dinner, Kraft.

Phone calls were far less reliable than text messages, so she didn't bother trying, their friend and savior Dylan Kane, a CIA Special Agent, rarely readily available.

Which could be a problem.

He might not get her message for days, and by then it would be too late. She hesitated.

Maybe you should try BD first?

She shook her head, the Delta operator even harder to reach.

Second.

She quickly typed a text message, giving the pertinent details in as concise a form as possible, then hit *Send*. She watched the indicator and it showed the message sent.

Then the screen flashed and went blank, the battery dead.

Oh no!

Pacific Coastal Region
Maya Highlands, Maya Empire
1092 AD

Something splashed on the ground in front of Captain Tai, some hitting his feet, the odor distinct though unfamiliar. Others around him growled in frustration as they too were hit by some viscous liquid, many taking direct hits. He looked up and saw one of their enemy high in the trees, pouring something out of a clay pot. He stepped aside as the thick substance hit the ground.

It had been a frustrating day, with his men falling prey to the far too clever traps and sneak attacks. He had little doubt that in a direct, head-on battle, they would be victorious, but this tit-for-tat battle couldn't be won, not in the long term. He had to assume his enemy had an unlimited number of men to throw at him, and he had but what Admiral Khong had brought.

He growled in frustration as he realized they were being doused with oil. This wasn't the way this journey was to have been. They were supposed to have been welcomed by the natives, embraced as the superior race, then showered with gold and jewels in thanks. They were to return to the empire laden with bounty, to be hailed as heroes who had proven the legends of this far off land once visited by their ancestors and almost forgotten to history.

He frowned as he spotted small fires ahead.

And cursed the ground he walked upon as his fate and those of his men were about to be sealed. He turned, pushing his men aside as he struggled back toward the boats, his heavy armor now a hindrance that could cost him his life.

Someone shouted and he glanced over his shoulder to see dozens of arrows, their tips afire, sail toward them, some embedding themselves harmlessly in the trunks of the surrounding trees, others hitting the oil-laden ground, flames flashing forth, engulfing his men. Their cries stabbed at his heart as he fled, shedding his armor as he tried to gain speed, painfully aware his own legs were covered in the flammable liquid.

And that this battle was lost, his only hope of survival to escape with the ships, then face the wrath of the Emperor for not only failing in their mission, but losing the Imperial Seal.

Grand Hyatt Macau
Cotai, Macau
Present Day

CIA Special Agent Dylan Kane stared at the woman lying across from him in bed, and frowned. She was gorgeous, sexy, and talented.

But he didn't love her.

Normally that wouldn't be a problem. In fact, it had never been a problem until recently. Now he was in love, in love with a woman his equal in every way, though right now, he felt so guilty, so ashamed, she was probably his superior in the ways that were important.

Lee Fang meant everything to him, and was the first woman to ever break through the barriers he had put up over the years to shield his heart from pain, and from inflicting pain on others, his job simply not conducive to serious relationships.

But Fang had changed all that.

She was Chinese Special Forces, knew the job, understood the sacrifices, and had made the ultimate herself—she had betrayed her country to protect it, now living in exile in Philadelphia, probably at this very moment waiting for him to return home.

And here he was in bed with a woman he had made love to all night. Unfortunately, that was the job—at least sometimes. He had slept with dozens of women—scores of women—over the years, many for God and country, most to drown out the pain of past transgressions.

Yet none since Fang had entered his life.

Until last night.

The job had demanded it. His handler had given him the target, told him to sleep with her so they could get compromising photos, photos that would be used to blackmail her into planting a bug in her brother's house, a brother well-connected in the Chinese Communist Party. He had seduced her easily, his charms effective, especially when a target had a penchant for Caucasian men.

It had been easy.

Too easy.

Many women wouldn't have cared enough about the photos to betray their family or their country. In this case, however, her brother was hoping to be the next First Secretary of the Chinese Youth League, and any suggestion his family was anything less than perfect, anything less than completely devoted to China and all things Chinese, could scuttle those plans. This poor woman had been used, and she would pay the price.

Yet he felt no guilt over that.

That was the job.

The reality was she had done what she did voluntarily, had definitely enjoyed herself, and for her indiscretions, she'd plant a bug that could never be traced back to her, and she'd be told the photos and videos were destroyed. The reality was Langley would keep them on file, his bare ass chewing up gigabytes of video in the storage servers back home.

Today, though, he did feel guilty as he stared at the bare back of this woman, picturing his trusting love lying in their lonely bed.

I can never tell her.

That much was obvious.

She probably suspects it, though.

He frowned. She knew the job. She knew what it could entail. But if they didn't speak of it, then he would never have to lie to her. Lies of omission were part of the job, yet an innocent question could shatter the delicate façade built up between their relationship and his chosen profession.

She knew enough to never ask him where he had been or what he had done, but pillow talk could be dangerous, especially when it came to matters of the heart.

Promise me you'll never break my heart.

It was something she had never said to him, though if she did, could he honestly make that promise? Every time he made love to another woman, he was potentially breaking her heart. If he were to slip up, or confess, he *would* break it.

Ugh. This is why agents don't have relationships.

Nobody to love, nobody to betray.

His CIA-issue watch sent a small electrical pulse into his wrist, indicating an encrypted message. He glanced at it then pressed the buttons along the sides in a coded sequence, a short message projected on the crystal. His eyebrows popped at what was shown, one of the encrypted messaging servers he had set up around the world indicating a message from one of the few civilians he had let into his life—the wife of his former university professor.

And they never contacted him for pleasure.

Something was wrong, and in mid-mission, there was little he could do to help, perhaps for hours, if not days.

Pacific Coastal Region
Maya Highlands, Maya Empire
1092 AD

Cheng Jun watched in horror as the fire spread, lighting the dark forest enough to see the silhouettes of his comrades as they writhed in agony, engulfed in flames. Some fled the carnage, though none escaped whatever was poured on them.

The battle was lost.

Though there was still time for revenge.

"Attack!" He rushed forward, his sword drawn, and swung, slicing open the back of the first unsuspecting enemy as the others turned, shocked at the ambush from the rear. They had the upper hand, they had the element of surprise, and they were winning the day as the enemy quickly fell.

One of his men cried out to his left, a spear embedded in his stomach, another to his right grasping at a hatchet in his chest, but the superior numbers of the enemy were proving no match for the close quarters combat of Cheng and his experienced troops.

Though as his force slowly dwindled around him, he noticed with a heavy heart that they hadn't been joined by the others supposedly on the right flank, apparently having fallen prey to the traps and ambushes of the enemy.

And with the main body afire, he and his men were all that was left of almost two hundred, and as he focused his attention on the young leader, surrounded by the last half-dozen of the enemy, he snarled, determined to avenge the death of his Admiral, and his comrades.

Balam Canek jabbed his spear through one of the gaps formed by his men, lancing one of the enemy in the arm, the man dropping back as Balam yanked his weapon free. They were now evenly matched, though in numbers only, and his loyal warriors, dying to defend him, were no competition up close with these demons.

He was going to die, like his father, his tenure as chief barely lasting a day.

Yet that wasn't his greatest regret.

That was reserved for Nelli.

The very thought of leaving her alone crushed him, and renewed the fight in his belly as he jabbed again, another of the enemy falling, though not before another friend died beside him.

And then he was alone.

The cries of the burning soldiers behind him filled the air, their screams growing fewer as the bulk of the enemy succumbed to their wounds. Now he faced five of them, alone, unscathed, their fierce eyes glowering at him, their horrific, grotesque faces snarling, leaving him to nearly tremble with the thought of what fate might await him should they take him alive.

He couldn't let that happen.

They inched closer and he thrust with his spear, swinging his ax as he readied himself. Someone shouted to his right and he smiled as the enemy spun toward the new arrivals.

It was his friend Kawil and the other banished refugees, surging from the trees, axes and spears held high as they set upon the enemy. He thrust forward with his own spear, plunging it deep in the side of one of the distracted enemy, as a wave of hope rushed through his body at the sight of his friend, at the sight of those his father had banished only yesterday, not content to let him die, but instead proving they were true members of their adopted home, true Mayans willing to risk their lives to save their own, unlike the cowards from the surrounding villages he had thought were his brothers.

If he survived this day, the gods be damned, these men and their families would be welcome at his table until the day he died.

South of Tepich, Mexico
Present Day

Acton stared at the jungle floor, picking his footing carefully, maintaining his balance difficult with his hands tied behind his back. The only advantage to the situation was that it was slowing everyone down. With three of the party bound, their captors were getting frustrated, the couple of times they had urged them forward faster, he had made a point of falling, delaying them even further. The longer it took them to reach their destination, the better.

He had a feeling death awaited them, not some long, drawn-out ransom negotiation.

He needed to give Laura time to get to the police and send help, and any delay could only benefit them—unless the men became too frustrated and decided any potential ransom simply wasn't worth the inconvenience. He hoped before any such frustrations might boil over, they would instead cut them loose to speed things up.

And if they made that mistake, it would at least afford him and the others the chance to escape, or to fight back when the authorities finally did arrive.

Laura had to be in town by now. It had been at least an hour since she had left. The students and the women would know where to go, all spoke Spanish, and by now she would have called their friend, and his boss, Dean Gregory Milton, a man used to contacting US and foreign governments on his behalf, Acton and his wife far too often getting into trouble through, in his opinion, no fault of their own.

Milton often begged to differ.

So absorbed by the math of calculating how long it would take her to reach town, find the police station, find someone who would listen, get them to organize a rescue party, then have that party arrive at the site, he had tuned out the conversation carried on by their captors. A stray word caught his attention and he listened.

"We should have told them to come back for us."

"Why? We had the trucks. If anything, *we* would be picking *them* up."

"Yeah, I guess. You know those idiots won't even notice we're not there. They'll dump the bodies then hit the first strip club they can find. They're probably already shitfaced."

Acton tensed. "What bodies?"

The leader, who he had heard called Diaz, looked at him. "The two trucks with our people and some of yours, I guess."

Acton stopped, his stomach flipping, his pulse pounding in his ears. "Are-are they dead?"

Diaz grinned. "Every last one of them. El Jefe doesn't want any witnesses to his operation."

Acton dropped to his knees, his mouth filling with bile as he struggled not to throw up. Reading knelt by his side, grunting from the effort of dropping to his knees without the benefit of free hands.

"What's wrong?"

Acton stared at the ground, his eyes burning as he translated for Reading. "She's dead. They're all dead." He bent over, his forehead hitting the cool ground as his shoulders heaved.

"What's wrong with him?"

Reading replied, his own rage and pain barely contained. "You killed his wife."

"Women are trouble. You're better off without her."

Acton rose, pushing to his feet with a roar, and barreled toward the man. Someone coldcocked him from the side, sending him to the ground. Reading crawled over to him, shielding him from any further blows.

"Save it, Jim, he's not worth it. Let's just get through this, okay?"

But Acton didn't care, for at this moment, he had no will to live.

Leroux/White Residence, Fairfax Towers
Falls Church, Virginia

CIA Analyst Supervisor Chris Leroux loved The Big Bang Theory. Penny and Leonard reminded him a lot of the relationship he had with his girlfriend, CIA Agent Sherrie White. She was way hotter than he was handsome, she had the street smarts while he had the book smarts, and they were madly in love.

And while watching a rerun not ten minutes ago, Penny had made mention of Leonard soaping her up in the shower. This had led to exchanged grins, a DVR put on pause, and a hastily run shower.

And lots and lots of soap.

He moaned as Sherrie cleaned and cleaned. He returned the favor though was too distracted to do it effectively. He gave up, leaning back against the wall, propping himself up with both hands.

His phone rang from the pocket of his abandoned pants, the coded ring telling him it was somebody too important to ignore. Sherrie recognized the pattern, standing and letting go of his apparently very dirty bits.

"I think he has a camera in here somewhere so he knows when to call."

Leroux took a nervous glance around, not putting the possibility past one of his few friends. He pushed the shower curtain aside and stepped out, water and soap soaking the floor as Sherrie tossed him a towel. He dried his hands then grabbed his pants, fishing out his phone and swiping his thumb. "Hello?"

"Hey buddy, it's me. Hope I'm interrupting something good."

Leroux glanced at Sherrie who pointed up, mouthing the word, "Cameras."

"Just, umm, watching some television."

"Uh huh, then why do I hear a shower?"

He thought quickly. "Oh, Sherrie's in the shower and I left my phone in here."

"Hi, Dylan!"

"Say hi for me, and whatever you do after this phone call, it better involve getting in there with her."

Way ahead of you, buddy.

He had known Kane since high school, he the geek, Kane the jock. He had tutored Kane and become friends, Kane his protector for two painful teenage years before leaving for college. They had lost touch, bumping into each other at Langley, rekindling a friendship that he valued almost as much as the one he had with the spectacular Sherrie, a relationship for which Kane was partially responsible.

"What can I do for you, Dylan? You rarely call to just say hello."

Kane chuckled. "You know me so well. Straight to business. I got a message from Laura Palmer. Looks like she and the Doc are in trouble again."

Leroux shook his head, these two archaeologists on his radar far too often. "What is it this time?"

"Looks like something in Mexico."

Leroux's eyebrows popped. "How the hell do you get into CIA level trouble in Mexico?"

"I don't know, ask whoever their puppeteer is. I got this message. 'Jim, Hugh, Prof Morales taken hostage by Mexican drug gang. Have their phone, mine lost. Many dead. Send help ASAP. Laura.'"

Leroux's eyebrows narrowed. "And that's it?"

"Yup. I've got the GPS coordinates from the metadata in the text message. I've tried calling back but it goes straight to some generic voicemail, so the phone is either dead, or she's keeping it off, perhaps so she can't be tracked by whoever's phone it is."

Leroux frowned. "You don't think she'd be dumb enough to try following them, do you?"

Kane grunted. "Dumb enough? No. Brave enough? Absolutely."

"One man's brave is another man's stupid."

"True enough. I'm on an op so can't do anything to help them. I've sent you the encrypted message. See what you can do, okay buddy?"

"Will do."

"Good. Now go help your woman in the shower."

Leroux blushed. "Umm, okay."

"Good boy. Don't forget to send me the photos."

Leroux glanced around for cameras. "Ain't gonna happen."

Pacific Coastal Region
Maya Highlands, Maya Empire
1092 AD

Cheng Jun spun away from the new arrivals, instantly recognizing they were about to lose. "Retreat!" he shouted, yet it was too late. His men were quickly felled by the overwhelming numbers. He ducked a blow, and rather than respond, instead raced toward the burning horde that had been his comrades. Sprinting as hard as he could toward what he hoped might be survivors, he reached the edge of the devastation, any hope of finding reinforcements lost, corpse upon charred corpse all he found, those still alive begging to be killed.

The massacre had been complete, the death from above a tactic he had never experienced before, and was certain never would again as he was unlikely to survive the day. His only hope now lay in the boats still offshore. If he could only reach the beach, he may yet survive, though the sounds of his pursuers continued to get closer.

He tore at his armor, tossing it aside as he ran for his life, for his homeland, for his family. Dreams of riches and glory were gone, now he only dreamed of the home he had left behind, now realizing he had already been a rich man, there no need for this journey at all.

He burst through the trees at the edge of the forest and onto the beach, the boats still offshore, their sails being raised. He spotted Captain Tai at the shore, struggling futilely to push one of the boats into the water. Another, filled with men, rowed toward them, though it was still several minutes away.

"Captain!"

Tai glanced over his shoulder, Admiral Khong's gold mask still in place. "Come! Help me!"

Cheng sprinted as fast as he could, slamming his shoulder into the boat, the pain surging through his body ignored as he grunted, the two of them slowly pushing the boat into the water. A spear embedded itself in the hull and he peered over his shoulder, all hope leaving his body as he spun, drawing his sword, placing himself between the enemy now encircling them, and his captain.

Yet it was futile.

They were defeated, even if the entirety of the skeleton crews left behind were to join them on shore. He closed his eyes and dropped his sword, tearing the stifling mask off his face and tossing it aside. He fell to his knees and opened his eyes, gazing upon the man clearly the leader of the supposedly primitive natives, natives who had soundly defeated a mighty imperial army.

And was shocked by the surprise on the man's face.

Municipal Dump
Tepich, Mexico
Present Day

Officer Hector Santana yawned then pressed deeper into the thinning seat of his police-issue SUV. It was nearing the end of his shift, and he was parked around the bend from the city dump, avoiding the public. Driving through town near the end of one's shift was an amateur-hour move—the risk was too great you'd get flagged down to deal with some petty dispute, chewing into your personal time.

And tonight his wife was preparing him his favorite, papadzules, a recipe thought to predate modern enchiladas, perhaps going back to the Mayans themselves—and he had no intention of being late.

She's too good to me.

And she was.

Even after twenty-five years of marriage, celebrated only three weeks ago, they were still in love. Four kids had grown and left home, all either in college or working in the city, all having avoided the temptations of the easy life offered by crime. He was proud of each and every one of them, especially young Julio, studying law on a scholarship program he had pulled a lot of strings to get.

He's going to change this family's station.

If Julio succeeded, which he had no doubt he would, his part of the family would forever be out of the slums, forever out of the constant struggle that was life in Mexico. Santana understood the appeal of running the border security gauntlet and trying for a life up north in the United States, but it had never held any appeal to him. He loved his country, his family was here, and he had made a good if simple life for himself.

He had a good job with the police department, and had managed to find a balance between refusing to be bought, and refusing to target the gangs. It was a fine line that kept him alive, his family untouched, and gave him the respect of those on the wrong side of the law, enough that when they saw him coming, rather than shoot, they instead packed up and left.

El Jefe and Galano had things tense in the town, though a truce had been maintained for several years now, his efforts at keeping the peace paying off so far. There was word of an altercation last week, but whatever had happened had been cleaned up by those involved before police had arrived, leaving only uncooperative witnesses.

This was one of the reasons he was sitting where he was. He had driven around the piles of trash, carefully eyeballing the tons of garbage in the hopes of spotting something, anything, that might suggest what had happened last week, the dump a popular cleanup spot for the gangs, bodies and other evidence far too often found months or years later.

Doors slammed nearby followed by some shouting. He checked his watch and sighed.

Three minutes until my shift is over.

Yet he had to check it out.

Nobody should be here at this time, which meant either scavengers, or those up to no good. Though technically illegal, if anyone were to successfully salvage something useful from the discarded waste of others, he personally had no problem with it, and if that was what was happening here tonight, he'd drive on, his mouth already watering at the thought of papadzules.

Though he had a feeling, a sinking feeling, that he wouldn't be that lucky.

He turned the key, the engine roaring to life, then put it in Drive, slowly pulling out from his hiding place and turning gently to the left, rounding a massive pile at the edge of the dump. Two trucks, one an SUV, the other a pickup truck, were parked, and two men were carrying something toward the nearest pile.

He stopped and climbed out, removing his shotgun from the rear gun rack. He pumped the weapon, the distinctive sound finally drawing the attention of the two men who turned and gaped at him, still carrying what was definitely a body.

No dinner for me tonight.

"Hola boys, what's going on?" One dropped the legs of their victim, reaching for a weapon. Santana squeezed the trigger, punching a hole through the man's chest, leaving him in a quivering heap waiting to die. He aimed the barrel at the partner, still holding the arms. "Care to join your friend?"

The body dropped to the ground with an unceremonious thump as hands were raised.

Pacific Coastal Region
Maya Highlands, Maya Empire
1092 AD

Balam Canek stared at the man, for it was a man. His face may have appeared slightly different, his eyes shaped oddly, yet it was those same eyes that told him all he needed to know.

This was a man.

This was a man who was scared, who was defeated, and who was finished fighting. The other, their leader, growled then leaped to his feet, charging at him. Four spears sliced through the air from behind Balam, their hurlers' aims true as all embedded themselves into the man's torso. He collapsed, his last gasps gurgles of tortured pain as he writhed on the beach, his bright red blood staining what had once been a beautiful, peaceful shore.

Balam knelt down and removed the leader's mask, again revealing the face of a man. There were no demons here, no gods, just men. He rose, showing the mask to the others. "See, he's just a man." He motioned toward the other of their enemy who sat on his knees, his hands clasped together, his eyes wide with fear as he clearly pled for his life. "As is this one."

"So they're not demons?"

Balam shook his head. "No, I don't think so."

The thick golden skins worn by the leader were tossed on the ground beside him, his men having picked up the discarded items in the forest. He kicked a piece with his foot. "Gold."

Shouts from the water drew his attention away from the defeated enemy, another group now approaching in a small boat, perhaps ten. He stared past them at what his mind couldn't fathom yesterday, yet today seemed so plain to him. A group of boats, massive, yes, but boats nonetheless. They were tied close together in the calm waters of the inlet, perhaps because the bulk of their crews were here, ashore, yet he couldn't take that chance. There could be hundreds more, and they were but a few dozen. He pointed.

"Burn them."

Dozens of arrows, their cohune oil-doused tips aflame, sailed overhead, embedding themselves into the decks and hulls of the clustered boats. The fires quickly took hold, and he watched as dozens of men desperately fought the flames, their efforts futile. Screams carried over the waves as those aboard burned or leaped into the water, abandoning their lost causes. The smaller boat had halted its approach, the men aboard now uncertain as to what to do.

I'll make it easy for you.

He pointed. "Kill them."

Dozens of tiny darts fired at the lightly clothed new arrivals, winces and slapped hands indicating his men's skill. Within moments all had slumped where they sat, the poison continuing to do its work. They were no longer a threat, and would be dead in good order.

He slid his thumb across his throat. "Kill any who reach the shore."

His men quickly spread along the beach in both directions, those swimming for shore no longer a threat, each now a mere individual against his small force.

The priest stepped forward, taking the lone survivor's chin in his hand, tilting the man's face from side to side as he examined him. "This is no demon, though he may be in the service of one. We can never really know for sure without sacrificing him. Should killing him bring rain, then we know our gods are pleased." The priest turned to Balam. "We should hold the ceremony tonight, before more can come."

Balam shook his head. "No. We must warn the others." He removed the green talisman from his pouch, the prisoner's eyes widening at the sight of it. "I will take him and this to Chichen Itza to warn the King. Everyone must know, should any like this attempt to land on our shores, that they should be stopped at once, for they do not have our best interests at heart."

Nelli and several of the women from the village emerged from the forest, and he stared at her for a moment, longing to hold her.

He turned to the priest. "You are in charge while I am gone. Should I not return, my brother shall be chief, as is his right upon my death. And should any more arrive, fight them should you think you can win, and if not, take the women and children to the other villages and let those cowards fight." He sighed as he took in the sight of too few of his warriors standing with him on the shore. "We have been victorious, but the price today was too high." He stared at the lone survivor. "Tie him up. We leave immediately."

Quintana Roo Cartel Lab #3
South of Tepich, Mexico
Present Day

Officer Hector Santana pulled to a stop, his headlights illuminating the small clearing, the light fading fast. Trees were flattened all around him, a large crater all that was left of what must have been a substantial drug lab. Bodies were strewn about, some killed by the blast, others burned beyond recognition.

All of it was exactly as described by El Jefe's man at the dump. Over a dozen bodies were in the back of the pickup truck. About half a dozen of them he recognized as local women, the others he had never seen before, but they were all young.

Too young.

They reminded him of his own children. He shook his head. What possible connection could they have with the drug lab? According to his prisoner, they had been found with their workers, so were executed, El Jefe having ordered the entire situation cleaned up.

And judging by the bodies scattered around, the job wasn't done.

Which begged the question, where were the others? Apparently, there were two SUVs filled with El Jefe's men, who had headed farther out of town to see where the unidentified young people had come from. He hadn't passed them on the way here, and it was unlikely they would have returned without finishing the job—El Jefe was not a patient man.

He sighed, many of the bodies clearly women, desperate women he knew only too well. He pulled out his satphone, the only one the precinct had, not trusting what he was about to say to go out over the police radio. He hit the speed dial, his call answered almost immediately.

"Hey Mariana, it's Santana. I'm about twenty kilometers outside of town. Looks like—" There was a burst of static then a man's voice cut in.

"Officer Santana, my name is Chris. I'm sorry to interrupt your call, but it's imperative that I speak with you."

En route to Chichen Itza
Maya Empire
1092 AD

Balam Canek sat near the fire, his legs crossed, his hands resting on his knees as he listened to the crackle, his eyes closed. His prisoner sat across from him, his hands bound, silent. They had made good time these past few days, and his prisoner seemed resigned to his fate, allowing Balam to relax slightly more with each passing sunset.

He opened his eyes and regarded his prisoner. Over the past several days of travel, he had nothing but time to examine the man. He was human in every way, just like him except for slight differences in the face, especially the eyes. Yet he had seen strange men in his time, men that appeared far less human than this one, and had treated them with respect.

And since the defeat of the demon army, he had been extremely cooperative, making no attempt to escape, and eagerly helping set up camp. Which was why he now had a much longer rope than when he started. A limited amount of trust was being established, but ultimately, the prisoner would die, though should he not attempt escape, it wouldn't be by Balam's hand, it would be by the priests in Chichen Itza.

When they arrived, he would be painted in the ceremonial blue, signaling his sacrificial future, prayers would be said at the top of the temple, then his head would be separated from his body, the blood offered to the gods as tribute. With the drought, he imagined there were many sacrifices, they always increasing in times of strife. Sacrifices were few in his part of the empire, his village fortunate.

A branch snapped behind him and he jumped to his feet, drawing his dagger. "Is someone there?" Another snap and his heart hammered.

"It's me, Nelli."

He sighed with relief as the woman he loved stepped out of the darkness and into the firelight. "What are you doing here?" he said, trying to be cross with her, yet failing miserably.

"I couldn't bear not being with you." She stared at him. "Are you mad?"

He smiled, grabbing her and holding her tight. "How could I ever be mad at you?"

"But it is against tradition. You are to take a wife from another village."

He smiled. "My mother spent many a night in my father's home. It is a foolish tradition that only works if one's love is not strong."

"So you still love me?"

"Until the day I die."

She buried her head in his chest and sighed, clearly pleased with his reply. She looked at the prisoner, tied to a tree with enough rope for him to be near the fire. "And him? Has he been a problem?"

Balam shook his head. "Not at all." He led her toward a cleared area around the fire. "Sit." Nelli sat, cross-legged, on the opposite side from the prisoner, and Balam handed her some water and dried meat. "Here, you must be hungry."

She nodded. "I didn't really think it through. I just left without telling anyone. I've been following you from a distance, but lost you after the first night. It's only by the will of the gods that I found your camp."

Balam stared up at the stars and said a silent prayer of thanks. "They must be pleased with what we accomplished."

She swallowed. "They must." She frowned. "But so many are dead. Surely they couldn't have wanted that?"

Balam shrugged. "I have no idea, that's a question for the priests. All I know is that when the gods aren't happy, they demand the blood of their subjects, and if the word from the east is true, then they must be very unhappy."

Nelli stared at the man sitting silently across from them, his eyes closed, his body turned away as if to give them some privacy. "Will they kill him?"

"Absolutely."

"If he was doing the bidding of his gods, then is he truly a bad person?"

Balam sighed, already having the same thoughts. If the gods had sent these men to punish his people for some wrongdoing, then this man and his comrades had been doing their gods' bidding. They had failed, and would be punished in the afterlife should that be their gods' will.

Yet did he deserve to die for this?

Probably not, though he had been witness to many innocents sacrificed over the years who had done nothing wrong, their only crime being unlucky enough to be picked by the priest when the gods demanded a tribute. Innocent people died for their gods every day. Why should this man be any different?

He sighed. He believed in the gods, though, like his father, had his doubts as to whether the priests truly were in communion with them, and whether they truly demanded so much blood in tribute. Yet to voice those opinions aloud would put one to the top of the list the next time a sacrifice was demanded.

If only I had the power to change the law.

Yet as a chief, he didn't. He could rule his people only in accordance with the laws handed down to them, laws interpreted by the priest, a man Balam had never trusted, though those suspicions could be from his doubts of the gods' desires.

"You're troubled, my love."

He smiled at Nelli as he snapped out of his reverie. "Sorry, I was just thinking."

"Of whether or not he should be sacrificed?"

He put an arm around her shoulders. "You know me so well."

"We should just set him free and disappear. Let's live together in the forest, raise our children away from all this fear and hatred and tradition. You're too young for your life to be over. Your father was never meant to die so soon."

Her words had appeal, of that there was no doubt, yet it would mean dishonoring his father, dishonoring his family. He placed his hand on the leather wrapped around the green talisman, eyeing the enemy sitting across from him, and sighed. "No, no matter how tempting that idea may be, we must warn the King. Never again can men like this be allowed on our shores, for surely it will mean our destruction."

Operations Center 3, CIA Headquarters
Langley, Virginia
Present Day

Chris Leroux pressed the earpiece tighter so he could hear better. He had called in his team after reviewing the scant details sent to him by Kane, little more than the raw text message. By the time he had arrived—his shower replaced by a mercy blue-ball recovery by his incredible girlfriend—his team had already located the source of the call, determined the phone was no longer transmitting, and had pulled Echelon records from the NSA, giving them a complete history from the moment it was activated a little over two years ago.

That intel had given them enough to know the phone was owned by someone in the drug business named El Jefe, located in Tepich, Mexico, which was less than twenty miles from where Laura Palmer's text message had been sent. A spy satellite over the area had spotted a police vehicle, the number on the roof used to track who it was assigned to, then a satellite call detected.

A satellite call he had his team intercept.

"Who is this?"

Leroux smiled, relieved the officer spoke English. "For now call me Chris. I need your help."

"This is a police phone! Do you realize how many laws you are breaking right now, señor?"

"Careful, boss, you could end up in a Mexican prison."

Leroux waved off Randy Child's snark, the young analyst brilliant but filter-free. "I am aware of that, Officer, however it's necessary. We have American, British, and Mexican nationals that are being held hostage in your area, with another British national of unknown status. We need your assistance in resolving this matter." There was a pause, Leroux watching the man as he stood by his truck, the phone pressed against his ear. An indicator in the corner of the display showed how many more minutes they had of satellite coverage, and it was rapidly winding down.

"Who is this? CIA? DEA?"

"Let's just say it is some three letter acronym. Are you willing to help us?"

Another pause.

"Perhaps. What is it you want to know?"

"Our understanding is our people have been kidnapped by men working for someone known as El Jefe."

There was a grunt. "That makes sense. I just shot one and arrested another a little while ago. They were dumping bodies."

Leroux frowned, signaling one of his analysts, Sonya Tong, to action that bit of intel. She immediately went to work. "Have you identified them?"

"No Caucasians, if that's what you're asking."

Leroux suppressed his sigh of relief. "Okay, understood. Do you have any idea why our people may have been taken?"

"Well, I'm standing at the edge of a crater that used to be a drug lab. I'm guessing they stumbled upon it somehow, and were caught in the middle when El Jefe's men came to clean up the mess."

Leroux frowned. That made sense. The Actons were do-gooders, always jumping into the middle of things they had no business getting involved with, though always with good intentions. Today, it just might cost them their lives. "Can you think of any reason why they wouldn't have killed them? Why they would kidnap them?"

"Ransom."

Leroux's head bobbed, along with most of the room. It was the going theory here, taps already put on all known Acton and Palmer accounts. "That's our theory as well. Listen, Officer Santana, do I have your permission to call you again should we need further assistance?"

"Sure. Maybe with you gringos involved, we might finally be able to take El Jefe down. But if you're going to do something, you better do it quick."

Leroux's eyes narrowed. "Why?"

"Because there's no reason to expect that when El Jefe finds out his men kept your friends alive, that he won't kill them immediately. He's cleaning up the evidence and wants no witnesses, and frankly, he doesn't need whatever ransom your people might bring him."

Leroux's chest tightened. "Thank you, we'll keep that in mind." He ended the call and turned to face the room. "We need everything we've got on El Jefe, the drug activity in the area, the police, and any local contacts we may have. And notify State. And the Brits as well."

"The Mexicans?"

"Let State deal with them. And no mention of our inside man. We don't want to get him in any trouble." He headed for the door. "I'm going to talk to the Chief and see if we can get some drones in the area. If they're on foot, they couldn't have gone far."

Chichen Itza, Maya Empire
1092 AD

Balam Canek stopped and stared, the sight before him overwhelming. For days they had traveled among thousands of others through the barren landscape, once proud farmland now parched soil, cracking and heaving, not even a weed breaking up the monotonous horror. He gripped Nelli's hand tight, the urge overwhelming to turn around and flee to the safety and blessings of their village.

"Come! You must hurry!"

He forced himself onward, their guide having already secured an audience with the King's advisors, the strange green talisman, and his tale of the great battle, enough to pique the interest of the court. He felt a tug on Cheng's rope, the man's name learned over their weeks of traveling together, a rudimentary form of communication now possible between them for the essentials.

He turned and his chest tightened at the horror on this man's face as he stared at a pile of bodies, all blue, all headless, discarded like refuse outside the city gates. Balam gently pulled on the rope and Cheng turned toward him, tears in his eyes.

Balam turned away, ashamed. "I'm sorry, I have no choice." He knew the man couldn't understand him, though his tone, he hoped, would be enough to convey the meaning of the words. Cheng nodded, and followed, his eyes directed at his feet as he tried to avoid the future foretold by the mass, open grave.

When they arrived at the palace, it was his turn to stop, the sight jaw dropping. Gold and jewels adorned the walls and ceiling, everything in the room a treasure, from cups to plates to knives. It was truly a sight to behold, the might of the King and the Mayan people proven by the opulence of the spectacle.

"Bow to your king."

Balam stared at their guide for a moment then finally spotted the living god. He dropped to his knees, Nelli beside him. He yanked Cheng's rope, forcing him to do the same.

"Rise."

He did, as did the others. The King stood, walking slowly toward them, the green talisman in his hand.

"This is a curious piece."

Balam kept his eyes directed at the floor. "Yes, sire."

"And you say it was taken from men like these." The King grabbed Cheng by the chin, examining him with curiosity. "Evil eyes," he muttered.

"Indeed, sire. At first, we thought they were demons, but after we defeated them, we realized they were men, perhaps only sent by demons."

The King grunted. "What do you think, priest?"

A man adorned in robes and gold stepped from the shadows, circling Cheng without touching him, as if afraid any evil he may represent might infect him. "He does appear to be a man, though unlike any I have seen before. You said they came in great boats?"

"Yes, sire, bigger than anything I have seen before, capable of holding dozens of men, if not more, along with supplies. And they had these huge, strange red wings. At first, I thought they were islands, they were so large, but my eyes were deceiving me."

The priest spun on his heel, facing the King. "There are tales of creatures such as this, with ships such as this, having reached our shores before, long before this city existed, yet these tales are so old, they are considered mere myth." He turned, regarding Cheng. "Though perhaps they aren't."

The King dismissed the observations with a wave of his hand. "I'm not interested in myths and superstition. These people came to invade my land, of that there is no doubt." He held up the talisman. "And this is obviously important to them, which means they could be back." He squared his shoulders, raising his chin. "Let it be known, that from this day forward, should any arrive on our shores bearing symbols such as this"—he raised the talisman high—"or with odd faces such as that"—he motioned toward Cheng—"they are to be met with deadly force. Under no circumstances can they be allowed on our shores, to wreak the havoc they may bring with them."

The official records keeper bowed, deftly recording the proceedings. The King held out the talisman and someone rushed from the shadows, taking it. "Now, put that in the library, along with an account of how it came to be in Our possession."

Balam pulled the bag off his shoulder, opening it. "Sire, you may wish to keep this with it."

The King's eyes narrowed. "What is it?"

Balam removed the suit of armor and mask that the leader had been wearing. "This was worn by their leader. It is rather distinctive, and may help identify them in the future."

The King nodded, a flick of the wrist sending someone from the shadows to retrieve the items. "Now, you must be tired and hungry after your journey. You will be my guests for dinner, and shall join us for the sacrifice of this one. Perhaps finally the gods will grant us rain and end the punishment we have endured for so long."

A crack of thunder echoed through the hall, the already dark skies throwing a mighty wind at them. Everyone rushed for the windows, staring out at the sky as the clouds opened up, releasing their bounty on a starving people.

Balam turned to Nelli, his mouth agape, the gods truly pleased. A hand squeezed his shoulder and he turned to see the King standing beside him, a broad smile on his face.

"This is the first rain we have seen in years, and they come with your arrival. The gods, I think, are pleased that you are here." He turned. "What say you, priest?"

The priest bowed. "The gods are indeed pleased." He motioned to Cheng. "The blood of this one may bring rain for a day, but"—he raised a bony finger and pointed it at Balam—"the blood of this one, one who has accomplished so much in their name, could bring us rain for a lifetime."

South of Tepich, Mexico
Present Day

Acton frowned as he tried to get comfortable, his head resting on a pile of leaves covered by his thin spring jacket, something he was thankful he had thought to don while waiting for the help Laura was supposed to have sent. He squeezed his eyes shut as he thought of the woman he loved, and the last time he had seen her.

But it was an imagined image.

The dust thrown up by the truck had obscured everything, his imagination creating the memory of her smiling and waving at him. She was dead, and it was because he had let her go with the survivors. He should have insisted she stay with them, though at the time he had assumed leaving the area was the safe choice.

He growled in frustration.

"What's wrong?"

He looked at Reading as the big man struggled to roll over without yanking on Morales who lay beside him, all three tied together at the waist, their captors having decided their bound hands were slowing them down too much. "Just thinking of Laura."

"Uh huh. Listen, it wasn't your fault. Leaving with the others was the smart choice based upon everything we knew at the time."

Acton sighed. "I know. But right now I'm in the mood to blame myself."

"You know who's to blame."

Acton glanced over at their captors, sitting around a large fire. "Yeah, I know."

Reading changed the subject slightly. "What are they talking about?"

Acton listened for a moment. "The ransom. They're wondering how much they're going to get."

Reading grunted. "I don't want any paid for me. Every ransom that's paid means another person gets kidnapped. I don't want that on my conscience."

Acton agreed. "Yeah. I only offered it to stop them from killing us. I had assumed Laura would reach town and send help." He shook his head. "Now I couldn't care less if they killed me or not."

"So no ransom?"

"Only if we all agree."

Morales rolled over, yanking Reading slightly. "Sorry, Hugh. I'll just add that I'd like to see my family again, but you're right. The cycle needs to be broken. Let's keep having them think they're getting paid. There are still good police in this town. When that many women don't come home for dinner tonight, their families are going to start asking questions. We may yet be saved."

"You're right. There's still hope." He glared over at their captors. "But they're not getting a damned penny of Laura's money."

Reading lowered his voice, leaning toward Acton. "I was thinking about something."

"What?"

"Who slashed their tires?"

Acton's eyes narrowed. "What?"

"Who slashed the tires? We were the only ones there. Everyone else left in the trucks. So who slashed the tires?"

Acton perked up slightly. "You don't think…" He shook his head, wishful thinking too often leading to false hope then crushing disappointment all over again.

"You know your wife. She's a survivor. She's been trained to react, not panic. You too. I've seen the two of you in action. If these guys ambushed the vehicles like they said, maybe she managed to escape and come back to try and help us. By slashing the tires and forcing them on foot, she probably saved our lives. We'd be wherever we're going by now, and probably dead."

Now *that* did make sense. Laura's head of security, a former British Special Air Service colonel, had been training them for several years in all manners of self-defense. And they were good. They weren't Delta good, though they certainly weren't civilians anymore. They knew their way around guns, knives and other ordnance, and hand-to hand combat was something they both excelled at, especially Laura.

And Reading was right. One of the most critical lessons taught to them was how to react in an emergency. While most froze, they had been taught to move. And with so many guns, knives, and grenades directed at them over the past few years, they had too many opportunities to put that training to the test. Sometimes he felt they had seen more combat than the average soldier today.

Which meant Laura would have reacted.

He smiled slightly, it no longer wishful thinking. "If she did survive, where do you think she is?"

Reading chuckled. "Knowing her, very close."

"Shut up!" shouted Javier Diaz, glaring over at the prisoners, one of them laughing. "If you're comfortable enough to be laughing, maybe I'll tie you up tighter!"

An apology was murmured, though it didn't sound sincere. Diaz didn't care, already feeling better about himself as the others laughed at his alpha male display.

"Do you think El Jefe will let us keep the money?"

Diaz stared at the youngest member of their group, Rivero, the question revealing his naiveté. "Ahh, no. But, if he does get paid, there'll be perks." This wiped the disappointment off the kid's face.

"Like?"

"Pucha! Lots and lots of pucha!" shouted Ybanez.

Grins rounded the fire.

Judging by the look on Rivero's face, women were a satisfactory perk. "I can live with that."

Ybanez elbowed him. "Ha! I bet you could. You probably haven't even popped that cherry yet."

The kid flushed, it apparently true. "Shut up. I bet I get more than you!"

"I'm married. You should!"

More laughter and Diaz leaned against the tree behind him, smiling as he thought of his wife and kids. He glanced over at the one whose wife had died by their hand earlier, and had to admit he felt a little sorry for the guy.

Though it wasn't enough that a few million bucks couldn't cure.

He chewed on his cheek.

Ybanez noticed. "What's wrong, Javier?"

He frowned, not pleased he had revealed something was troubling him. "There probably won't be any ransom."

Grumblings rounded the flames.

"Why not?"

"He doesn't need the money. *We* need the money, and you know El Jefe doesn't give a shit about us. If it serves his purpose, he'll keep them alive, but we were sent out today to kill all the witnesses, not take hostages."

"So you think he'll kill them?"

Diaz glanced over at the prisoners, the American staring back at him, probably having heard every word he said. "I don't think they'll last five minutes."

Rosa scratched her shoulder as she watched the woman named Laura, work at setting up camp. In the distance, they could see a large campfire casting a bright glow where the men they had been following had settled in for the night. The moment they had stopped, Laura had set to work, and it was impressive. She had found a large tree with a massive root system that gave them cover on three sides. She had swept it clear of debris with a bundle of sticks, then cut down dozens of leafy branches, laying them down as a floor for their tiny camp. She rigged up several branches and strung a large tarp between them at an angle, providing them with a roof over their heads, and more importantly, a fourth wall.

A small fire was lit and Rosa smiled, holding her hands over the flames, it now chilly. "Won't they see it?"

Laura shook her head. "No, their fire's too big. Their eyes will have adjusted so they won't be able to see this, not with the tree in the way."

"You're very smart."

Laura smiled. "Just experienced."

Rosa scratched her shoulder again. "Why are you following them?"

"One of them is my husband. The others are my friends."

Rosa took the sleeping bag handed her by Laura, thinking of her own husband. A wave of guilt swept over her. This was a good woman, trying to save the man she loved, just like she was. She worked for El Jefe only to put food on the table for her family, to buy medicine for her husband. She would do anything for them, including risking her life.

She hid the shame that threatened to overwhelm her, instead climbing into the sleeping bag and turning her back on the woman who had been nothing but kind to her. A tear rolled down her nose. She could have headed back to town after surviving the shooting, but instead had stayed with this woman, knowing that death awaited her should she return.

She had stayed with this woman for one reason.

She wanted El Jefe's men to capture them then reward her for her loyalty by letting her and her family live. She scratched at her shoulder again, the implant that would allow them to be tracked having gone unnoticed for months until now.

What I'm doing is wrong.

CIA Headquarters
Langley, Virginia

"Hi, sir, got a minute?"

The National Clandestine Service Chief for the CIA, Leif Morrison, glanced up from his desk, his eyes burning with fatigue. He checked his watch and frowned. "My God, is it that late?"

Chris Leroux chuckled as he stepped into the office. "Yes, sir, I'm afraid it is."

Morrison leaned back. "Speaking of the hour, what are you doing here?" He motioned toward a chair in front of his desk and Leroux dropped into it.

"I got a call from Dylan. Professor James Acton, Interpol Agent Hugh Reading, and a Mexican archaeology professor named Morales, have been kidnapped by a Mexican drug lord named Jesús Lepe, or El Jefe to those who love and admire him."

Morrison sighed, shaking his head. "Professor Palmer isn't mixed up this time?"

Leroux smiled. "Oh no, she is. She's the one who got the message to Dylan. We don't know what her status is at the moment, but knowing her…"

Morrison grunted. "Knowing her, she's in the thick of it. Okay, what do you need?"

"I've notified State of the situation and they're running with it. I'd like to put some feelers out to the Delta team that they know personally, to see if they can get themselves assigned somehow—"

"That's a stretch."

"Agreed, but there's been a lot of cooperation between us and the Mexicans in the drug war, so I figured it was worth a shot. Maybe they can get assigned as DEA advisors."

"Good thinking. What else do you need?"

"Drones over the area."

Morrison frowned, leaning back further, steepling his fingers in front of him, the tips tapping his chin. "That might be difficult. I'll see what I can do. In the meantime, go ahead and retask a satellite if you need to."

Leroux smiled. "Umm, already done?"

Morrison chuckled and pointed toward the door. "Get out of here before I have to reprimand you."

Leroux leaped to his feet with a smile. "Yes, sir!"

Fayetteville, North Carolina

"I think we may have overdone it a bit."

Command Sergeant Major Burt "Big Dog" Dawson squeezed his fiancée's hand a little tighter, concern written on his knit brow. "Do you want to turn back?"

Maggie Harris, the love of his life, and the first woman to truly capture his heart, shook her head, pointing instead to an inviting bench. "Just get me there and we'll sit for a while."

"I could carry you."

She stared at him. "There's only two times I want you carrying me. To the bedroom to rock my world, and across the threshold the day we get married."

"When I'll rock your world again."

She grinned. "I've heard wedding night sex can be disappointing."

Dawson's eyebrows shot up. "You've obviously never been married to me."

"Ha! Nobody's been married to you, so how would you know?"

Dawson channeled his James Bond theme songs. "Umm, nobody does it better?"

She patted his chest. "You may be Delta, but you're no spy. Now, Dylan on the other hand…"

Dawson feigned a mortal wound, clasping at his chest. "Oh, darlin', now I have to kill him, and I like the guy."

Maggie collapsed on the bench, breathing out a deep sigh. "In all seriousness, though, I was reading in one of my magazines that some experts say you should refrain from sex for one month before the wedding. That way you get some of the excitement back on your wedding night that you lost from all that pre-marital sex that's so common nowadays."

Dawson pursed his lips as he regarded her. "Umm, okaaay, I *guess* we could do that."

Maggie beamed. "You'd do that for me?"

"Babe, I'd do anything for you."

"Including not having sex for a month?"

Dawson nodded. "Sure, I'll let the Colonel know so he can deploy me to Syria. I'll singlehandedly take care of that little ISIS problem, come back, marry you, then make sure you never think of Dylan Kane again."

She grinned. "Deal!"

Dawson paused. "Umm, really? So you're serious?"

Maggie laughed, slapping his arm. "Oh, you men, you're so easy."

"This is true. The answer's always yes. Wait, what's the question?"

"There was no question." She leaned in and gave him a kiss. "Do you honestly think I could keep my hands off you for an entire month?"

Dawson breathed a sigh of relief, silently thanking God this had all been a joke. "I've never known you to be able to."

She rested her head on his shoulder and stretched her bad arm. "One of these days I'll be over this stroke, and we can get married."

He put his arm around her shoulders and squeezed her tight. Maggie had been shot in the head over a year ago, nearly dying, and had suffered a major stroke a couple of months ago. It had been a struggle, emotionally and physically, though she was finally making progress. Her speech was almost normal now, and she was up and walking, though only for short distances.

Her doctors, supplied by two of the most generous civilians he knew, James Acton and Laura Palmer, assured them that she would make a full recovery eventually. Yet that wouldn't be enough. Maggie had once had long, beautiful blonde hair. Most of it had been shaved off when she was first shot, and had nearly returned to enough of its former glory that she might entertain wedding photos with it, when she suffered her relapse, requiring the side of her head to be shaved again.

It was a crushing defeat for her, though she seemed to be coping with it better than before. The first time, she had refused to leave the apartment until her scar was at least covered. Now, she was unconcerned with the vanity side of things, and more concerned with reclaiming her life.

Which was fine with him.

She was the strongest woman he knew, and it was one of the many reasons he loved her as much as he did. She wasn't a quitter, and she wasn't a complainer. She had nearly given up a couple of months ago, but had soldiered through, and he was immensely proud of her.

He squeezed her tight as they sat and people-watched, soaking up the sunshine and fresh air.

"Hey, look who it is."

Dawson followed Maggie's gaze and smiled as Sergeant's Carl "Niner" Sung and Leon "Atlas" James jogged over to them.

"Hey Maggie, it's a perfect morning for a jog. Want to join us?" asked Niner, his body glistening with sweat. He jabbed a finger at the massive and chiseled Atlas. "I bet you can outrun this lug, he's slowing me down."

Atlas' impossibly deep voice rumbled a reply. "I'm like a juggernaut. If you get this much man moving too fast, it never stops."

Maggie giggled, always enjoying the friendly banter between the two men, both members of Bravo Team, a group of Special Forces operators led by Dawson, all members of what the public commonly referred to as the Delta Force, though in official circles they were 1st Special Forces Operational Detachment–Delta.

Maggie dug an elbow into his ribs and motioned at the two new arrivals. "Remember that article I was telling you about, where they're going to try a human head transplant?"

Dawson nodded. "Uh huh."

"Can you picture it?"

Dawson smiled, realizing where she was going with this. He stared at Niner then Atlas. "I don't know what would look more ridiculous. Niner's head on Atlas' body, or vice versa."

Niner stared up at Atlas. "Ugh. I'm afraid of heights. I wouldn't want to be up there."

Atlas regarded Niner with disdain. "I don't think I could take being so tiny." He leaned over and stared at Niner's crotch. "Everywhere."

Niner eyeballed him. "Hey, I might not hit bottom, but I'll scrape the hell out of the sides."

"Yeah, something only said by men with tiny—"

"Umm, lady present!" interrupted Maggie, waving her hand.

Dawson pulled his vibrating cellphone from his pocket. "Hello?"

"Mr. White, you're needed."

"Okay, thirty minutes."

"We need you sooner than that."

"Okay, fifteen." He ended the call. "Gotta go." He rose, holding out his hand to Maggie. "Let's get you back to the apartment."

Maggie took his hand and he pulled her to her feet. "Problem?"

"Something urgent at the Unit."

Niner took her other arm. "You go, we'll get her home."

Dawson looked at his friends then at Maggie. "You okay with that?"

"Sure, as long as they stop talking about their junk."

Niner grinned. "No promises."

Municipal Police Detachment

Tepich, Mexico

Officer Hector Santana stared at the temporary morgue set up in a back room of their humble police station. Over a dozen bodies from the two vehicles at the dump, then another couple of dozen bodies from the drug lab, had it appearing World War Three had broken out in his tiny town.

It had taken most of the night to transport all of them. The Federales had been called, and help was to arrive later today, though this place would be ripe well before that. The part-time coroner stood beside him, shaking his head.

"I've never seen anything like it."

Santana agreed. "From the tattoos, it looks like Galano's men hit El Jefe's lab. Something triggered an explosion, killing pretty much everyone except them." He pointed at the pile of women from the trucks—the ones he recognized. "They survived, somehow met up with these others"—he pointed at a second pile—"and they were all killed by El Jefe's men when they came to clean up the mess."

The coroner shook his head. "This is absolutely insane. So much innocent blood. All so gringos can stick needles in their veins to escape their problems." He spat. "They should try living here and see what real problems are!"

Santana grunted. "They might not be so quick to condemn us if they did." He unzipped one of the bags sitting on the autopsy table.

"With this many dead, will you finally be able to do something about El Jefe and Galano?"

Santana gave him a look. "What do you think? The judge already turned down my request for a warrant."

"Puta! Everyone in this godforsaken country is on the take." He paused, glancing at Santana. "Present company excluded, of course."

Santana smiled and bowed slightly. "Of course." He stepped forward, pointing at the shoulder of the woman on the table, a woman he recognized from his neighborhood. "What do you make of that?"

The coroner bent down and examined the small welt and frowned. "Almost looks like a smallpox vaccine scar or something, but very recent." He pulled out a scalpel and made a small incision then spread open the hole. "What the hell is this?"

1st Special Forces Operational Detachment—Delta HQ
Fort Bragg, North Carolina
A.k.a. "The Unit"

Command Sergeant Major Burt "Big Dog" Dawson walked past the empty desk usually manned by his fiancée, Maggie Harris. It was how they had met. She had her eye on him for apparently quite some time, and he was too absorbed in the job to notice it. It was the wives of the Unit that had urged her to take action, and she had.

He had been reluctant at first, his job, in his mind, too dangerous to risk leaving a family behind. A lot of the men in the Unit were family men, and yes, when tragedy struck, it was made all the worse when there were loved ones left behind, though it also meant there was a legacy. His decision to pursue the relationship—or more accurately, allow himself to be pursued—was one he would never regret.

He knocked on the Colonel's door, Clancy forgoing another temporary hire after the disaster that was the previous replacement.

"Come!"

Dawson opened the door and stepped inside. "Hiya, Colonel, you bellowed?"

Clancy grunted, motioning toward an empty chair, formality within the confines of these four walls strongly discouraged. "Looks like your professors have a situation again."

Dawson shook his head. He had first "met" Professor Acton when he had been sent to kill him. He had been provided with false intel naming Acton as the leader of a domestic terror cell that had already killed DARPA personnel transporting a top-secret project, and with plans to kill many more innocents if they weren't stopped. It had turned out to be all bullshit, and it was one of the greatest regrets of his life.

So many had died, his team used by a corrupt, madman of a president, and he and the others had sworn they would do whatever it took to make up for their actions, including helping out the unluckiest sonofabitch he had ever met. Acton was like a shit magnet, with every cult, madman, or terrorist seeming to be attracted to him or his wife.

They had kept him and his team busy, and as a result, had allowed him to not only learn to respect the professor, but earn his respect, and forgiveness as well. He actually considered the man a friend after all these years.

And if he needed help once again, he'd be happy to offer it, especially if it were on the books. The fact he was here, in the Colonel's office, suggested it was. "What have they got themselves into this time?"

"Looks like they stumbled into something in Mexico. All we know right now is that Professor Palmer got a text message to Dylan Kane stating that her husband, their friend Hugh Reading, and a Mexican professor had been taken hostage by a drug gang, that many were dead, and she needed help. Langley has confirmed there was an incident in the area, a drug lab explosion, and your friends are missing."

Dawson frowned. "If this is a ransom situation, they've got the money. If it were anywhere else, I'd say let it play out, but Mexico?" He shook his head. "Too many times they just kill them anyway." He leaned forward. "What's our government doing about it?"

Clancy shook his head. "Nothing in the way you're hoping. The Mexicans have agreed to send troops into the area to look for them, and have graciously agreed to four observers joining them."

Dawson grinned. "When do we leave?"

"Now."

South of Tepich, Mexico

Javier Diaz was bored, tired, hungry, and sore. They had been hiking for hours, but a poor night's sleep on the jungle floor with no food or water was taking its toll. He was in good shape, a necessity in his line of work. Guys with poor cardio or large guts too often found themselves dead, and he intended to live a long, fruitful life. He had worked his way up the ranks, now number two in the organization, and one day either El Jefe would retire—voluntarily or not—or he'd break away and form his own gang. He had ambitions, and ambitions needed money.

He eyed the American. He could be lying, perhaps just a pauper, though for some reason he believed him. He had hundreds of people over the years beg for their lives, bargain away their souls, but he could always tell when they were lying, and this one wasn't.

The question was how rich was he? It was something easily discovered once he got back to the compound and its Internet access. Within minutes, he'd know everything he needed about Professor James Acton.

He decided to kill the boredom. "Professor of what?"

Acton looked at him. "What?"

"You're a professor. Of what?"

"Archaeology."

"Is that why you were here? Some new discovery?"

The man hesitated to answer, suggesting whatever they had found was valuable.

Gold?

The thought excited him, and for a moment, he debated turning around. Enough gold and he'd be able to set up his own gang, no longer under the thumb of the terror that was El Jefe. "Answer or I shoot your friend." He motioned toward the other gringo, who sounded British to him. "What was in that temple?"

Acton exchanged a look with the Mexican who nodded.

Wise man.

"It was proof that the Chinese discovered America before Columbus did."

Diaz paused, turning toward him. "Are you serious?"

"Yes."

"Holy shit! That's incredible! Even here, we've heard about the Vikings, though I never believed it myself. How can you farm in Greenland? It's all ice!"

Acton replied, still appearing reluctant, though his enthusiasm for his chosen profession was winning over. Diaz could respect that, and it was an enthusiasm he missed, not having felt it for years.

I want to be El Jefe.

"The Vikings definitely settled Greenland and Newfoundland."

"Where's that?"

"Eastern Canada."

Diaz resumed walking. "The Vikings were in Canada?"

"Yes, about a thousand years ago. They've actually found the settlements."

"Huh, well I know Canada has a lot of snow, but not all of it, or least not all of the year, so I guess you could live there. But Greenland? That still sounds like bullshit."

Acton smiled slightly. "The Vikings settled there and successfully remained for several centuries. People tend to forget about the Medieval Warm Period. The world was a lot warmer a thousand years ago for several centuries. This made the southern portion of Greenland quite livable."

"So they had global warming back then?"

"Yes."

Diaz grinned. "I guess they were all driving Saabs and Volvos?"

Acton chuckled. "No, man had nothing to do with it, just like man had nothing to do with it all the other times it's happened throughout mostly unrecorded history."

"So what's different this time?"

Acton shrugged. "Depends on what you believe. Some say it's just because we have data now. But remember, when people say that the polar caps are the smallest they've been in recorded history, they mean since 1979. Data recovered from Shackleton's and Scott's logs indicate that when they were in the Antarctic over 100 years ago, the ice had receded just as much as it has now. We don't have enough of a record to definitively say what is happening today is any different than what has happened a thousand times before."

"So it's all bullshit?"

"I never said that. Climate change is happening, but it's happened before, long before we had a polluting industrial society. The question is whether or not what is happening this time is being made worse by mankind, completely triggered by us, or no different than any other time."

"El Jefe says it's just a scam to transfer money from the wealthy countries to the poor countries."

Acton shrugged. "Perhaps, though I doubt it. You have to look sometimes at who is pushing the message, and what they have to gain. If ex-Vice Presidents truly cared about the world, and were pushing the message for altruistic reasons, would they now be billionaires? Would they leave their SUVs idling while giving speeches? Would they buy property in San Francisco if it was supposed to be under water soon? If celebrity scientists truly believed we were destroying the planet, would they own multiple large homes? They'll claim they're buying carbon-offset credits, but what does that actually mean? I'll give ten kids cigarettes to smoke in China, but to balance it out, I'll take the cigarettes away from ten different kids in America? That way the net effect is zero across the planet?

"Bullshit. If you truly believe that we're killing our planet, then stop putting carbon into the atmosphere, period. Stop flying around in jets, stop driving around in gas guzzling SUVs, stop living in ten thousand square foot homes. Start living the lifestyle you're telling the rest of us to live, and stop stifling the voices of those who disagree. Do you realize it's almost impossible to get any funding now to study projects that might disprove manmade global warming? And if you do disagree, you're not only called wrong, you're stupid and evil, should be jailed, and you hate the planet and your fellow man."

"You seem to have strong opinions on it. You and El Jefe would get along well, I think."

Acton grunted. "Somehow I doubt it. And yes, I have strong opinions. I feel we should be able to openly discuss it and study it, and that hypocrites should be called out, even if they're right."

Something cracked behind them. Diaz froze, spinning on his heel, his eyes peering into the jungle. It had sounded like a branch snapping. "What was that? Was it one of you?"

A round of head shakes.

Ybanez jerked a thumb over his shoulder. "It came from behind us."

Diaz pointed at the three men bringing up the rear. "Go check it out." He watched them disappear into the thick trees, a frown etched on his face. Someone had slashed their tires and stole their satellite phone. That meant they had cojones.

And that meant they were too big a risk to leave out there.

Laura froze, staring at Rosa who stood cringing, her foot firmly planted on a dried branch. A branch now in two pieces. She looked toward the group they were following and could see several now heading their way.

Shit!

She turned to run, but stopped. It would make too much noise, and simply confirm the suspicions of those approaching. There was no way they could know for sure it hadn't been an animal or the wind that had caused the sound.

She searched for a hiding place and smiled, a large, dead tree stood nearby, the trunk partially hollowed out. She rushed over and peered inside, finding it empty, and large enough for the two of them. She signaled for Rosa to join her and the woman tiptoed over, carefully watching every foot placement. Laura urged her inside as she grabbed a leafy branch from another tree, hacking it off with her knife. She backed into the opening, pulling the branch over the hole behind her, then tried to catch her breath, everything now sounding amplified in the close quarters.

The three men rushed by her position, and through the leaves, she could see their heads pivoting in all directions as they searched for the source of the noise. One stopped, staring at the ground, apparently spotting something as the other two continued ahead.

If they find us, Rosa's definitely dead.

She slowly drew the large hunting knife she had salvaged from the camp and rose to one foot.

If I kill one, then they might kill James out of revenge.

She hated weighing one human life against another. There was no doubt her husband's life would always win out against a stranger, though it didn't make it right. But if she were captured, everyone might die, for she was the only one who could tell the authorities where her husband and her friends had been taken.

The man stepped toward their hiding place and bent over. The tree branch she was holding pulled away, and instinct made the decision for her. She lunged forward, plunged the knife into the man's throat, then twisted. He collapsed forward, gurgling in terror as Rosa sucked in a breath, about to scream. Laura slapped a hand over the woman's mouth, Rosa quickly replacing it with her own.

Confident she would be quiet, Laura let go and pulled her victim inside with them, quickly replacing the branch. She held a hand over the man's mouth, keeping him quiet as he slowly bled out. She could hear the others returning now and she prayed there was nothing outside that would reveal their cramped position. They walked past, talking rapidly in Spanish, apparently unaware their comrade was dying only feet away. She waited for a ten count then pushed the branch aside and stepped out, peering around to make certain they were alone.

They were.

She reached in and pulled the man out, quickly emptying his pockets. She stuffed his Beretta in her belt, a spare mag in her pocket, then with help from Rosa, rolled him back inside the hollowed tree and covered the entrance once again. She turned to Rosa. "We have to get away from here quickly and quietly. Understood?"

Rosa nodded, terror in her eyes, terror that Laura had a feeling was directed at her and not their common enemy.

Operations Center 3, CIA Headquarters
Langley, Virginia

"Sir, I've got Officer Santana from Mexico calling for you."

Chris Leroux's eyebrows rose slightly, surprised at Sonya Tong's announcement. He grabbed his headset and put it in place, nodding for Tong to put the call through. "Officer Santana, how can I help you?"

"Sir, we discovered something interesting here."

"What?"

"It's some sort of implant. All of the people we have examined so far that were working at the drug lab have had these things in their shoulders. I think it could be some sort of transmitter." Leroux smiled at Randy Child, hopping with excitement in his seat.

"You need to get me one of those!" he hissed.

Leroux agreed. "Please set a few aside for me. I'll have someone pick them up."

"Of course. When?"

"You'll be contacted shortly." He ended the call with a flick of his hand over his throat, Tong tapping her keyboard. He turned to Child. "What's the closest asset we have in the area?"

Child shrugged. "Delta is inbound. We could have them do the pick-up."

"Good idea. Contact their team lead and let him know. And make sure they've got the right equipment to pull the signal off those things.

If they don't, arrange rapid transport to our station in Mexico City. We need those frequencies now. We might be able to track it back to its source."

Staging Area

Valladolid, Yucatan, Mexico

Command Sergeant Major Burt Dawson hopped down from the UH-60M Black Hawk helicopter used to transport his team from the Mexican Air Base in Cozumel for their official mission as "observers". Though he had no jurisdiction here, and relations between Mexico and the United States were strained, he had no intention of sitting on the sidelines should the professors or Reading appear to be in danger.

Jurisdiction was irrelevant—he never had it when he was on a mission—and he couldn't care less about the relations between the two countries—things would work themselves out.

They always did.

A man dressed in the typical paramilitary fashion favored by Mexican Federales, strode up to them. "Agent White?"

Dawson extended a hand. "Yes, sir. Inspector Alfaro?"

"Si. Welcome to Mexico."

Dawson looked about at the staging area, there at least one hundred men gearing up, armored vehicles and several support helicopters evident. "What's the situation?"

Alfaro led them away from their chopper and the noise of the tarmac. "Everything is on hold. We're still waiting for the final approval to start the search."

Dawson frowned. "What's the holdup?"

Alfaro shrugged. "Who knows? It's this way all the time. Don't worry, we'll be moving by tonight."

Dawson stopped, bringing the entourage to a halt. "Tonight? We can't wait that long."

Alfaro waved a hand. "Don't worry, if your friends are out there, they're still in the jungle. There's no way they'll make it to town before nightfall."

Dawson's comm squawked in his ear and he held up a finger. "Just a second." Stepping away, he responded. "Zero-One, go ahead, over."

"Zero-One, Control. We've got a pickup for you. Details have been sent to your encrypted phone, copy?"

Dawson pulled his phone out and confirmed the message. "Copy that. Out." He scanned the message, disguising his curiosity. He walked back over to Alfaro and his men. "I need a vehicle."

Alfaro's eyes narrowed. "For what?"

"I want to visit my cousin who lives near here."

Alfaro eyed him then shook his head, a slight smile breaking out as he tossed him a set of keys. "Okay, just try not to kill your cousin or any of his friends. I don't need the paperwork."

Municipal Police Detachment

Tepich, Mexico

Officer Hector Santana sat behind his desk, wondering what he had got himself mixed up in. They were still waiting for the Federales to show up, and most of his fellow officers had called in sick, nobody wanting to be near the place with so many of El Jefe's people in the morgue.

They were scared.

And so was he.

It was already late afternoon, and he was desperate to get out of here, though felt it his duty to stay. He had managed to get home for a few hours of sleep and a shower, but it hadn't been enough. He was exhausted. And to add to his stress level, he had just received a call from the Chris person, obviously DEA or CIA, informing him that someone would be arriving shortly to pick up the transmitters.

The more he thought about it, the more he realized he should have kept his mouth shut and not told them about the devices. Forgetting the fact this person was American and he had no business telling them, these belonged to El Jefe. These were important to him, and he'd be wanting them back at some point.

He had no doubt that if things had gone as planned at the dump, El Jefe's men would have removed the transmitters themselves, but now dozens of them were here, including half a dozen in a plastic evidence bag sitting on his desk. If El Jefe found out he had given them to the Americans, he'd have him killed for sure.

You're a fool!

He was. He had got caught up in the moment, trying to do the right thing, shocked by the overwhelming violence that had taken place, the deaths of so many women he recognized and so many young people he didn't. He should have hung up the moment his call had been interrupted, yet he hadn't.

That at least was forgivable.

Calling them back was idiotic.

The chime at the front door sounded and he looked up from the transmitters. A man entered, walking on crutches, four kids helping him. Santana recognized the man from the neighborhood. "Señor Carona, what brings you here today?" he asked as he rose from his desk, noting the poor man's right foot had been amputated.

"There are rumors that some people were killed. My Rosa didn't come home last night."

Santana frowned. There was no keeping something like this a secret, which meant there was little doubt El Jefe's people knew by now. And if the transmitters were important to him, they could be here at any moment. But he had a job to do. "There was. A lot of people are dead. Did Rosa work at the lab south of here?"

Carona stared at the floor, unwilling to answer, that in itself an answer.

"No matter. She wasn't among the dead we found."

He brightened at this. "Then maybe she's alive!"

"Perhaps. But if I were you, I wouldn't tell anyone that. You know who's killing all the witnesses."

Carona's eyes widened and his children all hugged him. "Wh-what should I do?"

"Leave."

Carona's eyebrows rose.

"Do you have family you can go to? Away from here?"

He nodded.

"Then take the kids and get out of here. Today. Now."

Carona's shoulders slumped. "We will leave, but not before I know what happened to my Rosa."

"That's your choice," said Santana, holding open the door, "but it wouldn't be mine."

He noticed two SUVs pull up outside and wondered if it was the Americans arriving to pick up the transmitters. Eight men climbed out, locals. "Get out of here, now!" he hissed at Carona before slamming the door shut and locking it, warning the others brave enough to have remained. "We're about to be hit!"

Panic took hold for a moment as he rounded the front counter and grabbed the shotgun he had already prepared on his desk. The others were ready too, but they were outnumbered, two-to-one. Four men approached the useless glass door, machine guns held at waist level, the other four out of sight.

"There're eight of them. Looks like four out front. Watch for them coming from the rear entrance."

Roberto, a rookie, rushed up beside him. "Should we shoot first and take them by surprise?"

Santana smiled at him. "I like how you think." He popped up and took aim, knowing he might only get one shot at this. "I've got the one in the black hat."

"I've got the guy to his left."

"Fire."

Two thunderous shots echoed through the tiny police station, glass shattering, two of their attackers dropping. Santana pulled Roberto down as the other two emptied their mags into the front of the station, reloading several times as the walls and ceiling were shredded, the reinforced front counter holding for the moment.

Shots from behind them had Santana spinning to see what was going on. His fellow officers were taking turns firing down the hallway leading to the rear entrance, the others obviously already inside.

We're not going to last long.

He heard a cry as one of his friends took a round to the shoulder, dragged out of danger by the other, leaving only one man guarding their rear. There was a pause in the gunfire from the front, and he risked a look then fired, too late, both men diving to the side.

Steady fire erupted from behind him and he slapped Roberto on the shoulder. "Go help him!"

Roberto scurried away as Santana repositioned, his position exposed. Tires screeched outside and he cursed, more of El Jefe's men arriving. He glanced over at his desk, the photo of his wife and children missing. A moment of irrational panic gripped him then he spotted it on the floor, the glass shattered but the photo intact.

I guess I'll never enjoy your papadzules again.

Dawson threw open the door as he drew his weapon, the others doing the same. One of the gunmen spun around, his AR-15 spitting rounds at them, the passenger door taking a beating. Dawson fired twice, removing the man from the equation, Niner doing the same to the other, both hostiles dropping in heaps, their weapons silenced, though gunfire continued from inside the station.

He signaled for Atlas and Sergeant Will "Spock" Lightman to take the rear of the building as he advanced toward the front. A rapid series of shots he recognized as Glocks quickly silenced the remaining gunfire, an eerie calm settling over the area, civilians still scurrying for cover.

He poked his head through the door and heard a shotgun pump. "Hold your fire! American Drug Enforcement Agency! We're looking for Officer Hector Santana!"

"Th-that's me."

"Okay, we're friendlies, understood? I have two men at the back, and two in the front. Are you okay?"

"We have one wounded, but we're alive."

"Good. Now I want you to stand up and show me your hands." He peered around the corner and saw a forty-something police officer slowly rise, hands up, a shotgun gripped tightly in his right. "Okay, put the gun on the counter."

He complied.

"Okay, I'm going to come in. Does everyone understand?"

A round of "si"s was heard and he stepped inside, slowly, Niner just behind him and to the side, covering him. He reached forward and removed the shotgun from the counter, spotting the other three survivors near the back, their hands up as Atlas and Spock entered from the rear.

"Okay, we're all friends here, right?"

Heads nodded.

Dawson holstered his weapon, the others doing the same. He looked at Santana. "You have something for me?"

Santana shook out a nod then went to a desk. He retrieved a plastic bag from the floor then returned, handing it to Dawson as Atlas and Spock stepped through the shattered station and joined them at the entrance.

"Thank you. Can you handle things now?"

Santana shrugged, lowering his hands. "What choice do we have?"

Dawson frowned, wanting to stay and help these brave men, but he had a mission. "I guess not any. We'll be on our way now." He backed out then strode swiftly toward their vehicle when Santana shouted from behind him. He spun, reaching for his weapon when he saw the officer rush through the door, unarmed.

"Wait!"

Dawson walked toward him, his team taking up covering positions, watching for any approaching danger. "What?"

"There might be a survivor."

Dawson's eyes narrowed. He had been briefed on the drug lab explosion and the bodies, but this was the first he had heard of a survivor. "How do you know?"

"Señor Carona was here a few minutes ago. He said his wife worked at the lab and she never came home. She wasn't among the dead."

Dawson pursed his lips. It was an interesting possibility, though with the force of the apparent explosion, there might simply not have been enough of her left to recognize.

"Do you know what that means?"

Dawson shook his head.

Santana pointed at the plastic bag. "She will have one of those, too."

Dawson smiled, realizing what Santana was getting at. "Good to know." He pointed at the station. "If I were you, I'd get the hell out of there and wait for the Federales to show up. Whoever did this will probably send more guns."

Santana paled slightly. "Are the Federales coming?"

Dawson nodded. "Yes. But not until tonight."

Santana cursed, spitting on the ground. "Useless bureaucrats. We die while they fill out paperwork."

Dawson chuckled. "I hear you, my friend." He held up the plastic bag. "Thanks for this. Keep safe." He slapped Santana on the arm then climbed in the SUV, the others following as the officer ran back inside the station, hopefully preparing to abandon his post.

Some things were worth dying for, and a pile of dead bodies wasn't it.

Dawson handed the bag to Niner then started the SUV, pulling away, all the while watching for any new hostiles arriving. "See what you can get off of that."

Niner quickly went to work, the scanner already prepared. It took only moments. "Got it."

"Good. Send it to Langley."

Niner transmitted the frequencies to Langley through his encrypted phone. Dawson activated his comm. "Control, Zero-One. We've got your frequencies. You should be receiving them now, over."

"Copy that, Zero-One. We have them. We're tracking you now, so if you don't want the hostiles to know where you are, I recommend shielding them immediately."

Dawson grunted. "Roger that." He glanced in his rearview mirror as Niner snapped a lead-lined case shut. "Control, can you confirm you're no longer tracking us?"

"Confirmed, Zero-One. We'll get back to you as soon as we've completed our analysis."

"Copy that, Control. Be advised that our local contact says there might be a survivor with an active implant. We have no reason to believe she's with Acton or Palmer, but if she wasn't killed in the explosion, and was one of the survivors, she should have been in those trucks with the students. The fact she wasn't, and neither was Palmer, suggests she may have remained behind when the kidnapping took place. And if that's the case, there's no way Palmer would leave the woman to fend for herself. They just might be together."

There was a pause. It was a theory just pulled out of his ass, though it was at least remotely plausible.

"We'll look into it. Out."

Dawson yanked his seatbelt on, clipped it in place, then glanced at Atlas in the passenger seat. "I was thinking about what just happened."

"What?"

"Well, why were they attacking the station?"

Atlas shrugged. "Probably came to get the bodies, or at least see who was there and who wasn't."

Niner tapped the box with the transmitters. "Probably came to get these too."

Dawson agreed. "True. But think about it. Right now El Jefe's crew has no idea who's alive and who's dead. All they probably know is one of their labs blew up. They send a crew out to check it out, stumble upon the professors, kill all the locals, then bring them back to town to dump the bodies. But we know they didn't all return to town."

"How do we know that?"

"Because if they did, then who's Professor Palmer following? If she had a vehicle, she'd be near civilization by now and would have already called for help." He shook his head. "No, she's on foot, following them, which means they're on foot. We also know she has their satphone, so they have no way of communicating with the outside world, otherwise they would have just called for a pickup. And if they're on foot, El Jefe has no way of knowing who's alive and who's dead. The fact they just hit the station means they're looking for intel."

Atlas frowned. "If that's the case, it's only going to be a matter of time before someone thinks to check where all those transmitters are, if they haven't already."

Dawson cursed. "If there is a survivor with them, then El Jefe is going to know exactly where they are." He glanced in his rearview mirror at the others. "We might have just run out of time."

South of Tepich, Mexico

James Acton stumbled, quickly recovering his footing. He glanced over his shoulder and glared at the man who had shoved him. "Was that really necessary?"

"Go faster."

"Untie me and I'd be happy to." He glanced at Hugh Reading a few paces to his right, his face red with rage.

If he doesn't calm down, he's going to have a heart attack.

Reading was over a decade his senior, and though he may have packed on a few extra pounds stuck mostly behind a desk the past few years, he was no slouch. But this was rough terrain, and they were going through the thick of it. This was supposed to be a vacation, the three of them enjoying some downtime after so many run-ins with people hell-bent on killing them over the years, yet once again they found themselves at the mercy of men with guns.

Their only hope was whoever had slashed the tires, and he prayed every waking moment that that someone was Laura, though it probably wasn't. She was dead, along with the students and survivors.

"Hey, Javier, we didn't find anything. Probably just some animal."

Diaz nodded. "Well, we could hear you pretty much the entire way, so chances are you're right." His eyes narrowed. "Where's Jose?"

One of them shrugged. "Dunno. He isn't here?"

Diaz stopped walking. "No, he went with you."

Another shrug. "Haven't seen him."

Diaz growled, shaking his head. "Go look for him. We don't have any more time to waste." He held up a hand. "Wait. Give me the tracker." A tablet-like device was handed to him and he turned it on. "Shit! We've got a signal." He pointed to where the men had just come from. "Over there. One of the workers is following us." He tossed the tracker to one of them. "Go find her. Bring her here."

Acton's shoulders slumped as the two men departed. It was now confirmed Laura wasn't following them at all, but one of the workers from the drug lab. He sighed, his eyes burning as Reading stepped closer, having come to the same conclusion.

"I'm sorry, mate, but we knew it was a long shot."

Acton avoided eye contact. "I know. She's dead." His voice cracked. "Wh-what am I going to do?"

"Move!" A rifle butt delivered by Diaz slammed him in the stomach and he doubled over. "I want to get there before nightfall. Enough talking!"

Acton glared at him. "I'm going to kill every damned last one of you."

"Why, because we killed your wife?" Diaz grabbed Acton by the chin, squeezing it hard. "If you touch any of my men, I'll have your wife's corpse brought to me, and I'll slice her apart in front of you and feed her to my pigs."

Operations Center 3, CIA Headquarters
Langley, Virginia

"I've got it!"

Chris Leroux glanced up from his station at Randy Child's outburst, the young man—though barely younger than Leroux—pointing at the large displays curving around the front of the operations center. On the screen was an isolation of a map with a large cluster of pulsing red dots overlapping one another.

Leroux rose, stepping down toward the screen. "What am I looking at?"

"All the transmitters they're using. I was able to take the frequencies the Delta team sent us, decode the signal, then search for any other frequencies using the same encryption key." Child gestured toward the screen. "There you go, all the transmitters on the dead bodies."

Leroux smiled slightly. "Good work. Now zoom out, let's see if anyone else is being tracked." A few clicks from Child and the image zoomed out, several more clusters appearing, though only one drew his attention. He pointed. "Focus in on that one." Child complied, and the image zoomed back in, repositioning about ten miles to the south.

"That's not far from the drug lab explosion."

Leroux agreed with Tong's assessment. "Yeah. It's in between where Professor Palmer sent her text message to Kane, and the town where the bodies are. Can we get eyes on that?"

Tong shook her head. "Not likely. That's dense jungle."

Leroux tapped his chin then turned toward Child. "Do you have enough data yet to show what direction they're headed?"

Child nodded. "North." He gestured toward the screen and Leroux turned to see the image zoomed in much closer, a red line showing how the dot had traveled.

"What scale is this?"

"You're looking at about a quarter-mile in travel."

Leroux's head bobbed. "So enough to show a definite direction. What's in that direction?"

"Just the town."

Leroux pursed his lips. "Okay, that makes sense. It's probably the missing wife that Delta reported. She's probably trying to get home."

Tong spun in her chair toward Child. "Zoom out again."

Child spun the wheel on his mouse.

"Look. There's a road about two miles to the east. Why wouldn't she just take that? It would cut her travel time way down."

"And increase her chances of being caught. If it is the survivor, then she's scared and alone, and doesn't know who to trust."

"Can we assume she's alone?"

Leroux turned to Child. "Run with it."

Child chewed on his cheek for a moment. "Well, we know the bad guys ambushed the survivors, because they had a bunch of bodies and dumped them. We know they're linked to the professors, because she knows about the deaths. Remember, she said 'many dead' in her text. The unidentified bodies could have been with her group."

"That's true," interjected Tong. "According to what I've been able to gather, Professor Morales was leading a dig in the area with a team of students from his university."

Child repeatedly jabbed a finger at her. "That's right! So the students are probably the unidentified bodies. So if they were together somehow, the only explanation is that either the survivors came to the archaeological site, or the students went to the site of the explosion."

Leroux shook his head. "I can't see that happening. No professor in his right mind would allow his students to head to an explosion, certainly not en masse."

Child's head bobbed furiously. "Exactly! Which means the survivors came to the site."

"Do we know where this site is?"

"No, but we do know the professor's text message was sent from several miles south of the blast area."

Leroux stared back at the screen, their data points mapped out. "So, there's an explosion. It's close enough for those at the site to see. The students remain behind, and if I know our subjects, the professors and Agent Reading, and possibly Professor Morales, go to investigate. They discover the survivors and bring them back to the site. This now brings the students and the survivors together. They then leave together in two vehicles and are ambushed by the owners of the drug lab, looking to clean up the mess. This means they probably had a tracker with them so they knew where the survivors were."

Child spun in his chair, his head tilted back. "Right, but here's the thing. How did this one survivor escape?"

Tong shrugged. "She was never with the main group?"

Child shook his head. "No, they have the tracker, right? So they'd have used it to determine if anyone else had escaped."

Leroux stopped, turning toward Child. "She was with them when the ambush happened. They knew everyone they were looking for was together. They shot them all, or so they thought, but she escaped in the confusion. They never thought to check the tracker again, because they just assumed they still had everybody."

Child threw up his hands. "Bingo! I think we've got it. She somehow escaped the ambush, nobody knows she's out there, and now she's trying to get home."

Leroux sat, staring back at the screen. "So how does that help us?"

"Could she be with the hostages?"

Leroux shook his head at Tong's suggestion. "I don't think so. They'd have just killed her."

"Could she be with Palmer?"

Leroux's head tilted slightly to the side. "Perhaps, though there's no way to know." He rose and approached the screen. "We have no way of knowing where she is in relation to the professors, except it does provide a piece of data that we didn't have before."

"What's that?"

"We now know how quickly a person can travel in the jungle. If she's alone, then she'll probably be traveling faster than the hostages. If she's not, then she's either with them or Palmer, or she's being delayed because they're too close. Either way, we now have a worst case scenario estimate of when they'll reach their destination."

Child's eyebrows rose. "Which is?"

Tong tapped some keys, the image changing to show a large, walled compound at the edge of a town. "El Jefe's compound in Tepich. DEA says it's a fortress. About a hundred men on site, heavily armed."

Child whistled. "Christ, if they reach there, it'll take an army to get them out."

Forward Staging Area

Mahas, Yucatan, Mexico

Command Sergeant Major Burt Dawson tossed the keys to Inspector Alfaro who caught them easily.

"So, how's your cousin?"

Dawson smiled. "Still an asshole."

Alfaro laughed, shaking his head. He became all business. "You've heard where they think they're headed?"

Dawson nodded, briefed by Langley only moments before about the drug cartel's compound. "Yeah. Not a surprise. We should get in there before they arrive otherwise it's going to be a bloodbath."

"This is what I have suggested as well, however I've been overruled by Mexico City."

Dawson pursed his lips. "Come again?"

"The government feels there is no way to save your friends, therefore they are using it as an excuse to finally hit the compound."

Dawson tensed slightly, his blood pressure ticking up a few points. "You're telling me that the hostages have become sacrificial pawns in your drug war?"

Alfaro bristled, sniffing in a quick breath. "Not *my* drug war, Agent. *Your* drug war." He relaxed slightly. "Listen, we're all on the same side here, but we have different priorities. Yours is to save your people, ours is to save our country. El Jefe is extremely powerful, extremely well protected. The only reason we've been able to get any type of authorization to raid his compound is because of your people. If we rescue your people before they reach there, then there won't be a reason to hit the compound. By going in, full force, we can save thousands of lives. Your four people are unfortunately on the losing side of the equation."

"Uh huh. So shoot first, ask questions later."

"Yes. It's ugly, but that's Mexico today. Huge areas of our country aren't under our control, but thanks to your friends' kidnapping, we may be able to take a portion of it back." He lowered his voice, apparently picking up on Dawson's building rage. "Listen, we're going in and killing everything in sight. That's the unofficial orders from the capital. All of my men know about the hostages, and won't kill them intentionally, so there's still a chance they might survive."

"Assuming El Jefe doesn't have them killed the moment you open fire."

Alfaro shrugged. "That's always a possibility, but if we succeed in taking down El Jefe, they won't have died in vain."

Dawson suppressed a growl. "When are you hitting the compound?"

"Not until we know your friends have arrived."

"And how will you know that?"

"We've got eyes on the place now. We can see anyone coming or going."

Dawson spun on his heel.

"Agent, don't do anything rash. I can't allow you to risk this operation."

Dawson turned back toward him, stepping into Alfaro's personal space. He lowered his voice. "Those are my friends out there. You better pray they survive the night, or you and I are going to have a problem."

South of Tepich, Mexico

This isn't good.

Laura watched as the two men who had just returned to the group headed straight toward them. She ducked low, pulling Rosa down beside her, there barely one hundred yards between them. She rechecked the handgun she had confiscated, the magazine full with one to spare. She had killed their companion out of necessity, their location about to be discovered, but these two were an opportunity.

Killing them would leave only three hostiles, a much easier number than the original six, and the current five. Yet she had to be smart about this.

She shrugged off her backpack and took a nearly empty water bottle out. She held it up to her lips and drained it, then stuffed it with leaves, Rosa watching curiously. Laura pointed away from where the two men were heading. "Go that way and stay out of sight."

"Where are you going?"

"Don't worry, I'll be back."

Rosa nodded and scurried away, Laura cringing as she prayed the woman didn't reveal their position again. She turned back to watch the approaching men when they suddenly turned to the right. Matching Rosa's movements.

What the hell?

She hissed and Rosa turned. Laura signaled for her to stay where she was and rushed over at a crouch to join her. "They're following you. How?"

Rosa scratched her arm.

Laura grabbed the woman's hand and yanked it away, gasping at the fresh scar on her shoulder. She pressed her thumb into it and felt something hard underneath. "You've got a tracking device!"

Rosa's shoulders slumped and her face went red as her eyes filled with tears. Laura glanced over her shoulder, the men getting closer. They'd be on them in minutes, and with the implant, there would be no escaping them. Her hopes of an ambush were now impossible, not if she stayed with this woman who had betrayed her.

Just leave her.

With the device in her arm, and no time to do anything about it, Rosa was dead anyway. But if they chose not to kill her, they'd make her talk, and Laura had little doubt the woman would tell them everything she knew in an attempt to save her life.

Which would mean in short order they'd know she was out here, following them.

Laura looked again, the men getting closer, then back at Rosa, the terror and shame obvious. This woman was a victim. It wasn't her fault what had happened here today, and she could never live with herself if she simply abandoned her.

She sighed. "There's nothing we can do about it now." She pointed at the ground. "Stay right here." Rosa nodded and Laura quickly backed away, positioning herself behind a tree as the men continued to approach. She stuffed the barrel of the Beretta into her makeshift suppressor then pressed against the tree as they came into view. One pointed to the tree Rosa was behind, saying something in Spanish.

Just stay calm, Rosa.

The two men rounded the tree, barking an order. A trembling Rosa appeared, her hands held high. Laura stepped out from her hiding place, one hand gripping her weapon, the other holding the suppressor in place.

Yet she couldn't fire, she couldn't shoot someone in the back.

"Lads, if you would."

The two men spun toward her. She squeezed the trigger twice, putting two in the first one's chest, then adjusted her aim slightly, putting two more into his companion. They both dropped in heaps, their hands never reaching their weapons.

She tossed the suppressor aside, her creation at best a muffler, failing at reducing the volume as much as she had hoped. There'd be no hiding from the main group the fact that shots had been fired. She rushed forward, Rosa hopping up and down in a panic, two hands clasped over her mouth, her eyes wide.

Laura grabbed an AK-47 from one of the men then all their ammo, stuffing them in her backpack. She searched their pockets, a lighter the only thing of use. She picked up the tracker they had been using and pressed it against Rosa's arm. It beeped rapidly and the woman shrank away.

Laura dropped it on the ground then slammed the butt of the AK-47 against it several times, rendering it useless. She looked up at Rosa. "They can't track us now."

Acton's chest pounded from the adrenaline rush. Four shots had been fired, there little doubt of that. Their captors were now debating what to do, the three men clearly letting fear dominate their decisions.

"We should see what happened."

"I'm not going, no damned way."

Diaz silenced his two remaining companions. "Nobody is going. If they killed whoever was following us, they'll rejoin us. If they didn't, well…"

This silenced the two as they glanced nervously over their shoulders.

"Let's just keep moving. These constant delays will force us to spend another night out here, and I'm sick of this damned jungle."

Diaz pressed forward, ending the debate. Acton followed, with Reading close at his side, Morales behind them as the other two covered their rear, constantly watching the jungle for their friends.

They won't be coming.

"Did you hear the shots?" whispered Reading.

Acton nodded. "Yeah, two double-taps."

"Exactly. And from a handgun, not the AKs like those two were carrying."

Acton smiled slightly, Reading on the same page as him. "I'm guessing whoever is following us just took out two more of these guys, and is still alive."

"Yeah, and they might be well-trained."

Acton's eyes widened and he risked a glance at Reading. "Do you think it could be Laura?"

Reading frowned slightly, recognizing his desperate hope as just that. "No, Jim, I'm sorry, I don't. It's probably whoever blew up the drug lab." He leaned in slightly closer. "But whoever it is, just might give you the chance to get even with these bastards."

Forward Staging Area

Mahas, Yucatan, Mexico

"Remember when Agent K blew off that Tony Shalhoub guy's head in Men In Black, and it grew back, but was really small at first?"

Niner nodded at Atlas. "Yeah. Good movie."

"Well, that's what your head would look like on my body."

Spock cocked an eyebrow. "Are you two still going on about that?"

Niner shrugged, jutting his chin at Dawson. "What else are we going to do? He won't let me kill anything."

Atlas stared down at him. "We could spar."

Niner regarded him for a moment then shook his head. "Nah, I wouldn't want to embarrass you in front of all these fine Mexican soldiers."

Dawson grunted. "Uh huh. Sounds like a chicken shit excuse, to me." His comm squawked and he held up a finger, silencing his team, Colonel Clancy apparently finally reached.

"Zero-One, Control Actual. Status?"

"Sir, we're on hold here. The Mexicans are saying they're not going in until the hostages can be confirmed on the compound, then they intend to wipe everyone out. I get the distinct impression the lives of our people are of no importance to them."

"I see. And what do you want me to do about it?"

Dawson already knew there was nothing the Colonel could do to change the Mexican's minds, though there was one thing he *could* do. "We need to get in there first, sir."

"Sorry, Zero-One, you're there as observers only. When are they heading in?"

"They estimate the hostages should arrive by nightfall."

"Well, Zero-One, it sounds to me like you and your men have some downtime until then." There was a pause, a smile already creeping up Dawson's face. "Perhaps you should do some sightseeing while you wait."

Dawson outright grinned. "Yes, sir!"

South of Tepich, Mexico

Rosa stared at Laura as she dragged the bodies out of sight. This woman was unlike any she had ever met before. She was a killer. To call her a murderer might be accurate, though not fair. These were bad men who had taken her husband and her friends. If Rosa had the courage and the ability, she could see herself doing the same thing if it were her husband or children held.

Yet she was still terrified.

This woman seemed to invite trouble, to relish in it. She could have run away long ago, but she hadn't. She had killed three men by her own hand, and seemed determined to push forward, taking the weapons and ammunition off the dead, casually searching their pockets for anything useful.

It was chilling.

Yet some small part of her cheered this woman on. She was fighting back against the evil that was the drug gangs, gangs that dominated daily life in her small town, gangs that controlled her life—owned her life.

She was a dead woman walking, unless she could convince El Jefe she was still useful.

And this woman and her friends could be the key to that.

At least that was what she had thought at first. By keeping close to this woman, she had hoped to hand her over to El Jefe's men, yet she had never expected to be accompanying a female Rambo. There was no way she could overpower or trick this woman.

Yesterday that might have devastated her, yet today it gave her hope. This woman was incredible, a warrior, someone who might be able to help her. If she were on her own, she might get killed or captured before reaching the town, but instead, with this woman, she stood a chance of getting there alive so she could warn her family. Thanks to this woman, she might escape town before El Jefe found out she was still alive and ordered her family captured or killed.

And Laura kept saying that help was coming. She had sent a message on the now dead phone. If it had been received, help could be here any minute. If she were alone, or worse, if she had handed Laura over to the others, that help would treat her as an enemy. Certainly Laura would, should she betray the woman.

No, Laura was the key to saving not only her life, but her family's.

"Ready?"

Rosa shook her head and tapped the scar on her shoulder. "Cut it out."

Laura shook her head. "No, it's too dangerous. Besides, they can't track us now. We destroyed their tracker."

Rosa glanced at the glass powder on the ground where Laura had crushed the display, the remnants tossed into the bushes. "But what if they have another one?"

Laura paused then looked toward where the others were. "I only saw one. Did you see another?"

"No. But where we're going, they'll have many and will know we're coming."

Laura frowned as she stared toward the north, then at the scar. "Okay." She pulled her knife. "Any idea how deep it is?"

Rosa pushed her finger into the scar, the small hard nub just below the surface. "Not very."

Laura used the confiscated lighter to heat the blade and Rosa gulped, feeling weak. "Umm, you know what you're doing, right?"

Laura stuffed the lighter in her pocket and pulled out a Swiss Army knife. She handed it to Rosa. "Get the tweezers out. Small silver thing at the top."

Rosa pried the tiny device out. "This?"

"Yes. Now sit down, I don't want you collapsing on me."

Rosa sat, Laura kneeling beside her. "I'm going to do this quickly, okay. It'll hurt like a bitch, but it'll be over fast."

Rosa squeezed her eyes shut and turned her head away, realizing Laura had never answered her question. She cried out, slapping a hand over her mouth as Laura sliced at her arm. "That's one…"—another slice—"…and we're done."

Rosa turned to examine Laura's handiwork, the pain already subsiding.

"Tweezers."

Rosa handed them over.

"Okay, this is the worst part."

Rosa's eyes shot wide as Laura used her fingers to spread open the bleeding wound then reached in with the tweezers. Rosa gasped in pain, biting down on her finger as tears rolled off her cheeks.

"There's the little guy!"

And then the pain was over.

"Got it!"

Rosa opened her eyes and saw Laura holding the tiny device she hadn't seen since the day it was injected. It hadn't been covered in blood then, and she had never imagined it would hurt so much to have it removed. In fact, if she thought about it, no one had ever discussed how they would be taken out. It made her wonder if anyone ever survived long enough to worry about it.

Laura placed it on a rock then smashed it with the butt of her handgun. She cleaned the wound with some hydrogen peroxide from the first aid kit she had taken from the campsite, then taped a dressing over the wound. "There you go, good as new."

Rosa gently pressed against the bandage and winced.

Laura packed up the supplies then pointed toward the wound. "When we get back to town, we'll have that properly looked at. You might need some stitches."

Rosa nodded, wondering how she would pay. "Is that expensive?"

Laura grabbed her and gave her a hug. "Don't you worry about that, I'll take care of it."

Rosa smiled and returned the hug, feeling good about herself for the first time in months.

You chose the right side.

Operations Center 3, CIA Headquarters
Langley, Virginia

"We've lost the signal."

Chris Leroux spun toward Randy Child. "What?"

Child motioned toward the large display. "The signal's gone."

Leroux rose from his chair and walked toward the display showing the path the lojacked survivor had taken, the pulsing dot indicating an active signal, now gone. "Malfunction?"

"Doubt it. Those things are designed to last a long time."

Leroux's eyes widened as he turned back toward the others. "You don't think—"

"That they cut it out! Dude, that's sick!"

Leroux exhaled loudly, agreeing with Child's assessment. But what other possibility could there be? His eyes narrowed. "They still work if the subject is dead, right?"

Child nodded. "These ones do. Bodies in the morgue, remember?"

Leroux grunted, realizing his question was stupid. "Okay, something happened to kill the signal. If they were killed, then we'd still be getting a signal unless it was a miracle shot that hit the device."

"Unlikely."

"Agreed. So either it malfunctioned, or was disabled somehow." He stared back at the screen. "Either way, we know which way they're headed." He glanced over at Sonya Tong. "Any luck on the drones?"

Tong shook her head. "No, the Mexicans are still refusing. They've launched their own and said they'd let us know if they find anything."

Leroux frowned. "Lovely. So much for cooperation."

"I think they're pissed at us for some reason."

Leroux grunted. "Huh. I wonder what that could be."

Municipal Police Detachment
Tepich, Mexico

Officer Hector Santana stared at what had once been a small though efficient police station. Bodies were strewn about, bullet holes scarred the walls and furniture, and blood stained too many surfaces. Fortunately, they were all alive, the dead limited to those who had attacked them.

And there was only one reason for that.

The Americans.

Who they were, he had no clue. Probably some special DEA team. It didn't matter. They had saved his life, though probably sealed his fate. Too many of El Jefe's men were dead today, and he and the other police officers here would take the blame. No one would believe Americans had shown up and saved the day. They would be blamed for the deaths. He would be blamed for killing one and arresting another earlier.

And they had what El Jefe wanted.

The bodies.

They were obviously after the transmitters, just as the Americans had been. They had been excited by the discovery, and he wasn't certain why. These people were dead. Why would someone want to track corpses? He paused as he spotted a tablet computer held in one of the dead attacker's hands. He pulled it from the man's stiff grip and stared at the display. A cluster of red pulsing dots were shown, the overlay clearly of the police station.

And then it dawned on him.

There was obviously something that all these transmitters had in common, and if that information fell into the wrong hands, it could lead to every single drug lab El Jefe had.

He looked at the others, fear gripping him, for what he now held was the key to putting El Jefe out of business for good. And it was something El Jefe would stop at nothing to possess.

Nothing.

He gripped the tracker tight.

I'm already dead.

Forward Staging Area

Mahas, Yucatan, Mexico

"I hope Red starts shaving his head again. That damned fuzzy thing he's got going right now is freakin' me out. He looks like a tennis ball decked out for Valentine's Day."

Spock snorted. "Oh, man, he's so hearing that one."

Niner shrugged. "I can outrun him."

Atlas eyeballed Niner. "Not for much longer with those chicken legs."

Niner lifted one foot up onto a toe, twisting it and striking a pose worthy of a Paris runway. "These legs?"

"Those legs."

"You've been checking me out in the shower again, haven't you?"

Spock slapped his forehead. "You had to get him started."

Atlas waved his hands. "Don't be blaming me. He's always going there. The boy's confused."

"Not that there's anything wrong with that," added Spock with his best Seinfeld impression.

"Hey, I could give a shit which side of the vine he swings on, I'm just sayin', pick a side and move on."

Niner opened his mouth to defend himself when a large, black Chevy Tahoe rounded a corner, followed by a black sedan, both racing toward them. Dawson put a hand on his sidearm when the vehicles came to a halt. The door opened, and a man sporting government-issue sunglasses stepped out.

"You White?"

Dawson nodded and a set of keys were tossed to him.

"Courtesy Langley. There's a care package in the back." The man climbed into the idling sedan, its tires chirping as the driver pulled a 180.

Dawson tossed Niner the keys. "You drive."

Niner grinned at Atlas.

Atlas rolled his eyes and motioned toward the SUV. "This thing's as big as a boat."

"So?"

"They say women make better ship captains."

Spock spat the water he had just taken a swig of and Dawson clamped down on his cheek, trying to stop from laughing. As he closed the door, Inspector Alfaro rushed over, waving his hand.

"Where are you going?"

"Sightseeing."

"Again?" Alfaro eyed him for a moment. "You didn't happen to go sightseeing in Tepich earlier?"

"Why?"

"There was an incident at a police station."

Dawson shrugged. "Never heard of it."

Alfaro stared at him then pointed at his vehicle they had borrowed earlier. "Then how do you explain the three bullet holes in the door?"

Without missing a beat, Dawson replied, "You live in a very dangerous country."

"And you didn't think to mention it?"

Dawson shrugged. "I've been to Chicago. Felt like home."

Alfaro shook his head then came to a decision. "I can't let you leave with your weapons."

Dawson unclipped his holster, removing his sidearm. "No problem." He handed the weapon over followed by his MP5, the others doing the same. "I'll expect to get those back when we return."

"From sightseeing."

"Exactly." Dawson pointed ahead and Niner hit the gas, leaving Alfaro behind. "Let's go see where this El Jefe lives."

"I hear it's in a lovely part of town."

Dawson turned around to see Atlas and Spock going through the care package. "We good?"

Spock grinned. "Oh yeah, we good."

South of Tepich, Mexico

Acton tumbled, his foot catching on a hidden tree root. Reading reached out and grabbed him by the arm before he did a face plant, helping steady him.

"Thanks."

"You're lucky I have reflexes like a cat."

Acton gave him a look, suppressing a smile. "By cat, you mean Garfield, right?"

Reading chuckled. "With an attitude like that, I might just let you fall next time."

Acton opened his mouth to deliver his retort when he stopped, a voice slightly raised from Diaz, the tension in the air obvious among their captors. Three men were now missing, and it seemed pretty clear to Acton that they were dead. After all, if the shots they had heard were from Diaz's men, they'd be back by now.

And they weren't.

"Let's pick up the pace. We're only a few kilometers from the compound and I want to get there before dark."

Intentionally slowing these now scared men could get them killed, so Acton complied. He was still tied at the waist to Reading, Reading to Morales, but their hands and feet were free to facilitate their movements. The problem was they were too close together, and their enemy was separated. There were only three now. If he were to try and jump Diaz, there was no way Reading and Morales could get to the others—the rope was too short. They'd just end up yanking him away from Diaz.

His fingers casually ran over the knot then past it, not wanting to risk being caught. It was large and amateurish, which meant it would be difficult to untie. There was simply no way they would be overpowering these men as long as they stayed separate.

"I can't take it any longer!"

Diaz stopped, and they all turned toward one of the two men bringing up the rear. "What?"

"I have to know!" The man's eyes were wide, sweat beading on his forehead, his movements rapid along with his breathing. He was having a panic attack, which could make him dangerous. "Maybe we're moving too fast for them to catch up! Or maybe they're hurt!"

"Who cares?" replied his companion. "Less to share the ransom with."

"You fool, there's no ransom! El Jefe will just kill them as soon as we get there, then all of this will have been for nothing. They're slowing us down." The man glared at Acton. "We should kill them now."

Diaz chewed on his lip, his eyes drifting between the prisoners, the panicked man's words resonating.

And Acton couldn't let that happen.

"Did I tell you just how rich I am?"

Diaz paused, his eyes focusing on Acton. "No."

"Hundreds of millions of dollars. Even El Jefe will want his share of that." Acton stepped closer to Diaz, the rope tugging on Reading.

"Keep us alive, and after we're free, I'll personally make sure each of you gets a million in cash."

Greed spread with a smile across Diaz's face.

Santana Residence

Tepich, Mexico

Officer Hector Santana yanked open the door and stepped inside the home he had lived in for almost twenty years. It was humble, but it was his, containing all the memories of a life well-lived.

"Is that you, Hector?"

"Yes." He strode quickly through to the kitchen, the sounds of his wife already preparing food for him, echoing through the hall.

"I'll heat you up some dinner. It won't be as good as it would have been earlier, but at least it's something."

His nostrils twitched with delight from the smells of hours ago. But he shook his head, turning off the stove. "No, there's no time. Are you alone?"

Her eyes narrowed as she laughed at him. "What kind of question is that? Of course I'm alone." She eyed him. "What, you don't trust me?"

He grunted, shaking his head, there no time for humor. "No, I mean are any of the kids visiting?"

"No, of course not." She stopped. "What's going on? You're frightening me."

He pointed toward the bedroom. "Pack a bag. You're going to your sister's."

Her eyes widened. "What? No I'm not. I've got too much to do tomorrow. Besides, you know how she is with people just dropping by. She probably won't let me in the door!"

He took her by the arm and led her toward the bedroom. "Something happened. Something bad."

"What?" The fear in her voice was palpable, the realization that this was serious, finally taking hold.

"A lot of people are dead. A lot. And there'll be a lot more before this is over. I need you out of town so I know you're safe, and we don't have much time. The last bus for Mexico City is leaving in half an hour, and I want you on it."

She nodded, rushing ahead of him and grabbing their only suitcase. "What about you?"

"I'll be fine, don't worry about me."

She stopped tossing things inside the bag and turned to face him. "I want you to come with me."

He shook his head. "No, I might be the only one who can stop this."

Quintana Roo Cartel Compound

Tepich, Mexico

El Jefe sliced into his sixteen-ounce prime rib, the blood spilling out onto the plate, mixing with the garlic mash. He dipped the tip of his steak knife into the neat serving of horseradish and removed a generous helping, smearing it on the meat. He bit into it and chewed, closing his eyes as he moaned in ecstasy.

Rita giggled and he opened his eyes before swallowing. He stabbed the air with his fork, pointing at the steak. "There's nothing like a good, rare steak, grilled just right."

Rita took a dainty bite, moaning herself, giggling like the airhead she was. She was perfect for her purpose. A convenient place to park while the wife was away. He frowned. She'd be back tomorrow, and chaos would return to the household—chaos he didn't need, not with the trouble Galano was causing him.

But she was the mother of his children, so he couldn't just kill her, not without hurting his daughters, and if there was one thing he couldn't stand, it was seeing tears in their eyes. They were the best part of him, and he loved them dearly. He just hoped they grew up to make him proud.

Otherwise, he'd have to slit their throats.

The door burst open and his tech guy, Rayas, stormed in, his face red, sweat pouring down his forehead, his portly frame swaying side to side as he rushed toward the table.

"Rayas, you've gotta drop a few tons or you're going to have a heart attack."

"Si, señor." Rayas eyed the food, distracted from his purpose.

"You interrupted our dinner to stare at my steak?"

Rayas tore his eyes away. "No, um sorry, El Jefe, but we just got a call from one of the cops on our payroll. Our guys sent to hit the police station are dead. All of them!"

El Jefe rested his hands on the table, still gripping his utensils as a rage built within. "How?"

"Don't know. Somebody showed up. Maybe Federales."

"Are they still there?"

"No. They spoke with Santana then left. Santana left as well, but he took the tracking tablet."

This put El Jefe over the edge and he leaped to his feet, the chair skidding across the floor as he whipped his knife at the wall, the blade embedding itself deep into the plaster. Rita yelped, curling up into a ball in her chair. El Jefe pointed at Rayas. "Send everyone. I want them all dead. And I want those damned transmitters." He lowered his voice to a growl. "And find Santana and bring him to me. I want to kill him personally."

South of Tepich, Mexico

Laura listened as a heated discussion took place between her husband's captors, dissension clearly in the ranks.

Probably wondering what happened to their three buddies.

She glanced over at Rosa, hiding behind the tree next to her. "Can you hear what they're saying?"

Rosa nodded. "He says he wants to know what happened to their friends."

Exactly like I thought.

The group structure was breaking down. That could be good, though it could also be bad. The less unified they were, the easier they might be to take on, but it could also lead to rash actions, not the least of which could be the killing of the hostages.

And if that were to happen, she'd never forgive herself.

She closed her eyes, fighting the burn.

If they die because of what I did…

"One is coming!" hissed Rosa.

Laura opened her eyes and saw one of the men heading their way, angry words tossed over his shoulder at the others. The leader dismissed him with a wave of his hand then turned around, resuming their trek.

Laura's mind raced as she watched the clearly agitated man storm toward them. She had little time to act, and in her overconfidence, had closed the gap with the others too much. Shooting him this close would invite pursuit by his friends, or at least heavy, sustained gunfire that could hit her or Rosa. It might also create the tipping point where they could kill the hostages so they could run away faster.

But if they're left to wonder...

If they were left to question what had happened to him, they might push forward, human nature to hope for the best when scared, not necessarily leading to the right decision. She and Rosa could hide, and let this one live, yet it would mean losing the golden opportunity to thin the ranks by one more.

She glanced over at Rosa, the poor woman terrified, her eyes wide, her chest heaving. "Do you know how to use a gun?"

Rosa shook her head.

"It's easy." She handed her the Beretta she had liberated earlier. "This is the safety." She flicked it. "It's off. If something goes wrong and he comes at you, just point it at his chest and keep squeezing the trigger until he stops." She smiled. "And make sure you keep your eyes open. You're more likely to actually hit something." Rosa shook out a nod, staring at the weapon with horror. Laura pointed toward the trees to the right. "Hide in there. You'll be okay."

Rosa stumbled toward the cover, the gun gripped loosely in both hands. Laura reached into the backpack and removed a length of yellow rope looped into the tarp. She tied several overlapping knots in the center then coiled the rope around both hands, giving it a good tug to make sure it was secure.

This will be a first.

She pressed her back against the tree, the sounds of the approaching hostile now loud, the man apparently making a point of stepping on every branch he could, the noise perhaps giving him a false sense of security, evolution wiring humans to think loud noises scared away predators—and today she was a predator.

Yet there was a flaw in his logic.

Human predators were rarely scared by loud noises.

He was only feet away now, walking quickly, clearly hoping to find his friends soon so he could return to the safety of his comrades. It would be his downfall. She spotted Rosa through the trees, the woman shaking like the leaves that surrounded her.

And if she could see her, then so could her prey.

She signaled for her to get farther back and Rosa nodded, fading into the background.

A branch snapped and Laura cringed.

Her target stopped, saying something in Spanish, his tone suggesting a question.

There was no reply.

His weapon appeared, held out in front of him as he inched toward Rosa's position. If he were to fire blindly, he might hit the poor woman.

She had to act now.

She stepped out with purpose, her hands raised high over her head, then dropped them down before he could react. She pulled the knot tight against his throat and spun, using her back as leverage to pull his feet off the ground as her hands crossed over her head. He struggled, his feet flailing in the air as he rocked back and forth, but she kept pulling as hard as she could, battling to maintain her balance, his superior weight threatening to bowl them both over, and if that should happen, he could break free.

She tipped to the right and shoved her foot out, stabilizing the struggling load, grunting from the effort as the battle behind her changed, the hands flailing against the rope weakening, the stifled shouts turning to gurgles, the attempts to wrest free, fading.

And then he went limp, a final sigh escaping his crushed windpipe, the knot having served its purpose. Laura collapsed to her knees, exhausted, but continued to hold on tight. Finally she let go, shoving one shoulder up, rolling the dead weight off her and onto the jungle floor. She cringed when she saw his face, his eyes bulged, his tongue sticking through his lips, his neck bloodied and bruised. She felt for a pulse and found none.

He was dead.

Rosa appeared from the bushes, the weapon pointed at her, Rosa's hands still shaking.

And the look in her eyes had Laura wondering just what the woman's intentions were.

Bus Station

Tepich, Mexico

Officer Hector Santana hugged his wife hard, trying to appear as calm as possible though it didn't matter. His wife was panicked. "You need to calm down," he whispered in her ear and she nodded, her entire body still trembling. "Call me as soon as you get to your sister's, okay?"

"Y-yes."

"Okay, now go." He gently pushed her toward the door and she stepped onto the bus, turning back to give him one last look. He smiled at her, trying to convey all the confidence he didn't feel. She blew him a kiss as the doors closed, the driver impatient at the delay. Santana watched as the bus pulled away, the center of his universe walking down the aisle, her eyes still on him until the bus turned the corner and she was out of sight.

He sighed, closing his eyes as he struggled to control his hammering heart.

Please, God, keep her safe.

He spun on his heel and headed for his truck, his eye catching the station manager on the phone, staring at him.

And any confidence he had that his wife would be safe, left him.

South of Tepich, Mexico

Rosa's hands trembled as she gripped the gun in both, aiming at this woman who absolutely terrified her. She stared at the body of the man she recognized from town, his face a contortion of bulging flesh, his neck torn apart, his killer standing over him, her chest heaving from the effort of her cold-blooded deed.

She was a maniac.

Four were now dead, one from a knife in the throat that had soaked her in blood, the stains still evident on her clothes. Two by expertly fired shots, shots fired through a plastic bottle, something she couldn't imagine anyone except a trained killer knowing how to do.

But this, this latest act, had been gruesome beyond compare. To strangle someone to death—to know *how* to strangle someone to death, was something Rosa had never thought anyone she would actually meet in person could know. Certainly not a woman.

She's mad! She's dangerous!

Her eyes focused on the tip of the gun, the barrel bouncing around as she struggled to steady her aim, her trembling hands and hammering heart making it impossible. She could shoot the woman and end it all. She could still fulfill her original plan. Before, she had thought there was no way to overpower this woman, but that had all changed the moment she was given the gun.

She had the power now.

All she had to do was squeeze the trigger. Squeeze the trigger and it would all be over.

She'd call for the others and they would find her, and she'd be rewarded. She would be allowed to live, and so would her family.

Right?

It would happen that way, wouldn't it?

"Look at me."

Laura's voice startled her, Rosa forgetting that there was a human at the other end of the barrel for a moment. She tore her eyes away from the gun, staring at the woman who had her so frightened.

Just squeeze the trigger and you'll save your family.

"Rosa, I need you to calm down and lower the gun."

Rosa's eyes returned to the weapon, now shaking even more.

Kill her and it's all over.

Her shoulders tensed as she inhaled with a gasp. She held her breath and closed her eyes, her finger squeezing slightly on the trigger.

You'll never be able to look your children in the eyes again.

She cried out, tossing the gun to the side, tears bursting forth as her shoulders shook. Arms enveloped her as the taller woman embraced the one who would have her dead.

"It's okay, it's all over."

How could she be so forgiving? How could this woman, who a moment ago she was about to kill, be so caring? "I-I'm sorry. I'm just so scared. I have a family. I-I just want to live. I want them to live."

Laura squeezed her tight, a hand patting Rosa's head. "I'll tell you what. When we get out of this, I'll move you and your family anywhere in Mexico that you want. Deal?"

Rosa stared up at her, a wave of hope rushing through her. "You can do that?"

Laura nodded, a gentle smile on her face as she wiped Rosa's tears away with a thumb. "Yes. Would you like that?"

Rosa's head bobbed rapidly, already picturing returning back home, away from this godforsaken town.

"Then do we have a deal?"

Rosa smiled. "Yes."

Route 295

North of Tepich, Mexico

Esperanza Santana gripped the handle on her suitcase, her knuckles white, the rigid edges digging into her legs unnoticed. Her breathing was rapid, her vision narrow, her eyes focused on the back of the driver's head, her mind not registering what it was, just a random point in space it had decided was the least threatening thing around her.

The bus was about half-full. Most were asleep, though there was no possible way that awaited her tonight. She closed her eyes.

Calm yourself or you'll have a heart attack.

She pictured her father, dead in his bed, a massive heart attack taking him in his sleep when she was a child. It ran in the family, and she worried it would one day take her, or worse, one of her children.

A car engine revving behind the bus distracted her. Tires squealed and headlights sliced through the dusk beside them as a car raced past them, waking several of the passengers. The bus driver cursed as the car cut in front of them. Brake lights lit and the distance between the car's bumper and the bus narrowed rapidly. Another curse followed by a prayer erupted from the driver as he slammed the brakes on, tossing the unprepared passengers against the seats in front of them, Esperanza fortunately already bracing in anticipation.

Angry shouts were silenced as all four doors of the car opened, the occupants stepping out, the headlights of the bus giving everyone a clear view of the men responsible.

Men with guns.

Esperanza's hands gripped the suitcase even tighter as she sucked in a breath, holding it.

"Open the door. Now."

The driver complied, the doors opening with a hiss, his hands rapidly shooting up. Two of the men boarded, the first facing the passengers, the other keeping a gun pointed at the driver.

"Which one of you is Esperanza Santana?"

Esperanza shrank in her seat, lowering her head behind her suitcase. Footsteps slowly approached.

"Show yourself, or I start killing."

Her pulse pounded in her ears and she felt dizzy. Her held breath escaped with a gasp as she rapidly drew in lungsful of air. She was going to die. They were here to kill her.

Which meant they had probably already killed her husband.

She glanced at the terrified passengers sitting across from her, a woman and her little daughter, cowering in fear.

No one will die because of me.

She held up her hand, still crouching behind her suitcase. "I-I'm Esperanza Santana."

South of Tepich, Mexico

Laura picked up Rosa's discarded handgun and shoved it in her belt, quickly searching for anything useful on her latest conquest's person, finding nothing of value. As she did so, she kept a wary eye on Rosa, not sure if she could trust her anymore. She could understand the woman's fear. She had been indoctrinated into a society of criminals that valued loyalty and silence beyond all else. When something went wrong, they silenced all who could expose them, as was evidenced by the ambush on her and the others in the trucks. There were no questions to be asked before shooting, or after. They wanted everyone who could link them to the drug lab erased, and Rosa was evidence.

In her panic, she could tell the police what she knew before returning to the frame of mind where she remembered her life depended upon her silence. El Jefe obviously wasn't willing to risk survivors keeping their mouths shut when they were emotional. Rosa knew she was dead, and probably had thought that she might save her life if she delivered her boss the only other person to escape the ambush. It would prove her loyalty, her sanity, and Laura had to admit, if any one thing could save Rosa's life, it would probably be that. Yet there was an equal chance he would thank the woman then kill them both, regardless.

But Rosa now had an option.

An option she hadn't had when she insisted on sticking with her. She had a way out for her and her family. The question was would the promise of freedom be enough to overcome the fear she had been living under for so long.

Laura slung the AK-47 over her shoulder and turned to Rosa. "Ready?"

Rosa nodded, her mood slightly brighter than a few minutes ago. Laura pressed forward, wishing she had eyes in the back of her head as Rosa followed. She had to get over the distrust and focus on what lay ahead, otherwise she might walk into a trap. There were only two hostiles left, and if she got lucky, she just might free everyone before they reached the town.

She glanced over her shoulder. "How much farther?"

Rosa shrugged. "I don't know, I've never been through here, but it can't be much farther."

"And you're sure we're headed toward the town?"

Rosa pointed up at the sun, low on the horizon, only slivers of it visible through the thick canopy overhead. "We've been heading toward town the entire time." She pointed to their right. "The road is only a couple of kilometers from here. I think they're scared someone might see them, so they took this route."

"Any idea where they'll go when they reach town?"

"They're probably going to El Jefe's house. It's like a fortress. If you want to save your husband and your friends, you'll have to do it before they get there."

Laura frowned. Judging by how far she estimated they had walked over the past two days, she figured they couldn't be more than an hour away from town. She might have to act soon. There were only two hostiles left now, and they were in a hurry, probably scared they would die next.

Give me the chance, and I'll make sure you do.

Municipal Dump

Tepich, Mexico

Officer Hector Santana sat in his SUV, out of sight as he tried to figure out what to do. His phone vibrated on the passenger seat and he picked it up. He pressed the *Talk* button and put it to his ear. "Hello?"

"We have your wife."

His entire body tensed as he held his breath, recognizing El Jefe's voice. He gripped the steering wheel as he battled to maintain control. "Why? She's done nothing. *I've* done nothing."

"We both know that's not true. Bring me the tracker or she dies."

Santana closed his eyes, his shoulders slumping. "She's dead anyway. So am I."

"Perhaps. But it's *how* she dies that should concern you. She's a little old, but she's a fine looking woman. I think the boys here might like to show her a good time."

Santana opened his eyes, his grip on the steering wheel tightening as his upper lip curled. "You lay a finger on her and I'll kill you."

El Jefe laughed. "That's the spirit! If I don't see you within the hour, she's meat for my men."

Operations Center 3, CIA Headquarters
Langley, Virginia

Chris Leroux stood in front of the large display, his hands on his hips as he watched a convoy of vehicles leave El Jefe's compound. The Mexicans had thus far provided them with only cursory updates on what the drones were showing—essentially that the hostages had not yet arrived, and little else.

Leroux was having none of that.

It hadn't taken long for his team to hack the feed. They could now see everything the Mexicans were seeing, the only limitation was they had no control over the drones. They could take over if they wanted to, though that would tip the Mexicans off to the hack, and perhaps cause a diplomatic row.

"Do we have sat coverage?"

Sonya Tong tapped at her keyboard, another display showing the feed. "For ten minutes."

"Okay, make sure we see where that convoy is headed."

"Yes, sir."

Randy Child cleared his throat. "Maybe this would be a good time to hit them?"

Leroux shook his head. "No, Acton isn't there yet. The Mexicans won't move until their excuse to assault the compound arrives, and we have no idea when that will be." Leroux glanced over at Tong. "Get me

Delta." A few key presses and whispered words before a nod. Leroux adjusted his headset. "Zero-One, Control, be advised we have a convoy of a dozen vehicles leaving the target compound, heading east, destination unknown, over."

"Copy that, Control. Do we have eyes on the compound yet?"

"Affirmative, Zero-One." He snapped his fingers, pointing at Child who nodded, his fingers attacking his keyboard. "We're patching you into the Mexican drone footage now."

"Copy that. So they decided to cooperate?"

"I wouldn't go so far as to say that."

"Understood, Control. Okay, confirmed, we now have the footage. Do we have any intel indicating any change in our expectation that our targets will be coming from the south?"

"Negative, Zero-One, no change."

"Copy that, we'll find a position with a good view of the southern approach. And you're still sure they're not already there?"

Leroux glanced around the room, everyone shaking their heads. "Affirmative, Zero-One. There's no chatter, and our satellite coverage has shown no indication of that, though we don't have constant coverage."

"So they might have arrived during black-out periods."

"We don't think so. The Mexicans have had constant drone coverage, and they haven't moved yet."

"Good point. Keep us posted on that convoy. That's a lot of mobile firepower, and I don't want it surprising us."

"Roger that, Zero-One. Control, out."

En route to Quintana Roo Cartel Compound
Tepich, Mexico

Headlights bounced ahead, approaching fast. Officer Hector Santana cranked the wheel of his truck, pulled down a side street, then gunned it as he watched his rearview mirror. A dozen vehicles sped by, there little doubt where they were coming from.

Or where they were going.

They were probably heading for the police station to finish the job the others had failed at. But they'd find nothing except their prisoner, still locked in his cell. The officers and staff had left to wait for the Federales to arrive, Federales who despite repeated phone calls, kept pushing back their ETA. They were obviously up to something big, or El Jefe's tendrils ran far deeper than even he thought. Could he truly be powerful enough to stop the federal authorities from responding to a massacre this large?

He pulled a three-point turn, slowly returning to the main road leading to El Jefe's compound, wishing he owned his own car, his police vehicle a beacon in a town where tonight, being a police officer meant death. If the Federales didn't get here soon, there wouldn't be a police officer left alive.

Including him.

He glanced at the tracking device on the passenger seat. As soon as he handed it over, he was dead, and so was Esperanza. Nobody would be left alive, their deaths, and those of his fellow officers, a message to the replacements—keep out of El Jefe's business, or the same happens to you.

He stopped at the end of the side road, checking both ways, seeing no one. The only way anyone was surviving was if the Federales showed. They were the only force large enough to stop El Jefe, the tiny police detachment inconsequential.

His eyes widened slightly at a thought. There was another force large enough, large enough to challenge the stranglehold El Jefe had on his town, especially now that so many had left the compound undefended.

But it meant making a deal with the Devil.

He turned left, away from the compound, already praying for forgiveness.

Outskirts of Tepich, Mexico

James Acton peered through the trees ahead and frowned. The glow he hadn't been sure was there minutes ago, was now obvious in the rapidly darkening surroundings. And it wasn't the moon. They were approaching the town, which meant their fate would soon be decided. Their only hope was if El Jefe had any interest in the millions Laura's money could bring him, and that interest could be heavily influenced by these men he had offered a million each in cash.

"There it is!" cried Diaz, quick thumping hugs exchanged. Acton looked over his shoulder at the jungle behind them, wondering who it was following them, and if they even had any interest in him or the others. Whoever it was had killed four so far, all bad guys. But that was purely because they had left the strength of the group. Their pursuer could simply ambush them and kill everyone. There was no reason to suspect whoever was following them had any motivation other than killing El Jefe's men. This wasn't some sort of stealth hostage rescue.

As soon as they were behind the walls of the compound, they at least stood a chance of negotiating with El Jefe. But if they were to remain out here, they could be killed any moment by whoever was after them. The idea of dying didn't bother him. He had been overwhelmed with a rollercoaster of emotions over the past day, knowing that the only woman he had ever really loved was dead. In fact, he couldn't care less if he died.

He glanced at Reading to his right. He had a son. And Morales had a wife and several children. They deserved to live, to see their loved ones again. And so did he. He may have lost Laura, but his parents were still alive, and no parent should have to outlive their child. And he had friends. And his students. His eyes burned as he realized he had a lot to live for. It would just be hell living it without Laura. But she would want him to go on. To survive this ordeal, and to honor her memory.

He drew in a deep breath and squared his shoulders as he spotted the corner of a building through the trees, now determined to survive.

And with no idea how.

Rosa pointed at several lights ahead and wisely kept her mouth shut. Laura nodded, dropping to a crouch beside the woman. "I see it." She could hear the others just ahead, perhaps a hundred yards, though without going in, guns blazing, she could see no way to stop them. "How far is it to the compound?"

Rosa stared at the lights then pointed to the left. "It's just over there. Very close."

Laura cursed.

Too late.

"Okay, we can't stop them now. We'll have to follow them, then I'll call for help."

Rosa pointed to the right. "I live that way. I can go home and call."

Laura considered this idea for a moment. She still didn't completely trust the woman who less than an hour ago had held a gun on her, yet what choice did she have? If Rosa was going to betray her, staying together would probably make that more likely, since all she had to do was call out. If she left and betrayed her, El Jefe's men would know nothing beyond what they already knew. Somebody was following them and had killed four of their men.

She frowned. No, they'd know something else. They'd know *who* had killed their men, which could mean her husband and the others could be killed in retaliation. But if she trusted the woman, she could keep an eye on things, perhaps take advantage of some lapse that might let her free them. If her message had been received by Kane, then help might already be here, simply waiting for an update as to where everyone was.

And if he hadn't, well, no amount of phone calls would matter.

And that was a risk she couldn't take.

She had to continue to follow the others, in the remote possibility there was something she could do. She stared into Rosa's earnest eyes, and took a leap of faith. She pulled a pen and piece of paper from her backpack, quickly writing down Greg Milton's number, the only person she could think of who might be able to help them quickly. "Call this number and ask for Greg. Tell him that you're calling on my behalf, and that Dylan"—she wrote the first name down—"knows what's going on. Tell him where we are, okay?"

Rosa nodded, taking the paper and stuffing it into her pocket. "Good luck, señora."

Laura smiled. "You too."

Rosa turned to leave then stopped. She grabbed Laura and hugged her hard. "Thank you for saving me."

Laura squeezed her eyes shut, a sense of relief surging through her as she realized this woman could be trusted. "You're welcome."

Rosa pushed through the trees, quickly disappearing, leaving Laura to wonder if the poor woman would even make it to her home alive.

Galano Residence

Tepich, Mexico

Officer Hector Santana trembled, hopefully imperceptibly, as he stared at the second most powerful drug lord in the region, Antonio Galano, sitting behind a large, antique desk, a cigar clamped between his teeth, a scotch held delicately to the side, gently swirled as one vice was exchanged for another.

"What brings you here so late, Hector?"

"I have a problem."

Galano smiled, holding both vices out to either side as he looked at his men. "Well, I'm known in these parts as a problem solver." His men chuckled. "Tell me what your problem is, perhaps I can help."

Santana sucked in a long, slow breath, steeling for what he was about to do. This was a crossroads in his life, and the moment he asked for this favor, everything would change. "El Jefe has my wife, and he's going to kill her."

Galano's head bobbed before taking another sip of his scotch, the ice clinking against the crystal. "That *is* a problem. But why should I care? You're a good cop, Hector, and good cops are of no interest to me unless they get in my way." He leaned forward in his chair. "Or decide to become bad cops." He stabbed the air between them with his cigar. "Are you ready to become a bad cop?"

Santana tensed, playing his one card. "No."

"Then I think you're wasting my time." Galano flicked his wrist, dismissing Santana, his henchmen moving closer. Santana took a hasty step forward.

"Wait! I have something you want."

Galano waved his hand, his men backing away. "What?"

"I have El Jefe's tracker."

Galano's eyes narrowed. "What tracker?"

"One of the ones he uses to track all of his lab workers."

Galano's eyes widened slightly as he rose from his chair and leaned forward, his knuckles pressed into the wood. "Now just how did you manage to get your hands on that?"

"There was an incident. His men are dead. I took it off one of the bodies."

Galano stood. "Show it to me."

Santana shook his head. "Do you really think I'd be stupid enough to bring it with me?"

Galano smiled, grinding his cigar into an ashtray, putting it out. "No, I suppose not. What do you want for it? Money?"

Santana shook his head. "My wife."

Galano laughed, the others joining in. "And just how the hell do you expect me to get your wife from him? I assume she's at his compound?"

Santana nodded. "But there's something you don't know."

Galano's eyes narrowed. "What?"

"I just saw at least fifty men leaving there. They're going to the police station. If you hit him now, there'll be almost nobody there."

Santana recognized the glimmer in Galano's eyes and pressed his advantage, stepping closer to the desk. "Get my wife, and the tracker is yours. You'll know the exact location of every single drug lab he has in the country, and you'll be rid of him once and for all."

Tepich, Mexico

Rosa rushed through the streets of her new home, every voice, every laugh, every bark of a dog sending her heart racing even faster. She kept to the shadows, terrified if someone recognized her that a call to El Jefe might be placed. She had no way of knowing whether they knew she was alive, but if they did, she had no doubt word would already be out, a substantial reward offered for her capture. And in these parts, with everyone so desperate to survive, a hefty reward from El Jefe could change lives.

She ducked down the alleyway behind her home, not trusting to use the front door. If El Jefe were watching the home, that's where she suspected they'd be. She froze.

But wouldn't they cover the back, too?

She stared into the dimly lit alley, the dusk sky providing little light, and saw no one. She had to risk it. She walked as calmly as she could the last few feet then opened the back gate, wincing as it creaked, the hinge unoiled in years. Before today, it had been a security feature, its opening never going unnoticed. Today, it was a dead giveaway to anyone who might be listening for it.

"Rosa, is that you?"

It was Señora Villas next door. She ignored her and yanked open the back door, stepping inside quickly before closing it.

"Mama!"

Little feet stampeded toward her, crying out in excitement.

"Shhh!" She held a finger to her lips, trying to silence them, yet it was no use. She sighed when her husband appeared.

"Where have you been?"

She shook her head. "No time. I have to make a phone call. Everyone pack a bag. We're leaving tonight."

Milton Residence

St. Paul, Maryland

"I'm going to call Washington and have his damned passport revoked."

Sandra looked up from her eReader at her husband. "Can you do that?"

Gregory Milton shrugged. "I don't know. I'm the dean of a university. That's gotta count for something in this world."

Sandra reached over and patted his hand. "Only in your little corner of it, dear."

Milton gave her a look. "Sure, kick a man when he's down."

Her eyebrows rose. "Didn't know you were."

He sighed. "I just wish I knew what was going on. It's been two days since I've heard from them. I can't reach any of their phones, and the university says they haven't heard from Morales either."

"Well, he did mention it was a new discovery. Maybe there's no cellphone coverage."

Milton shook his head. "No, there's no answer on their satphone either."

Sandra sighed at him. "Like I already told you, the battery is probably just dead. You're worrying about nothing."

Milton dropped his head forward. "Umm, you do know who we're talking about, right? Jim Acton? The world's greatest magnet for trouble? Movies should be made about what that guy gets himself into."

Sandra waved her eReader. "Books too!"

Milton grinned. "Yes, books too." He sighed, trying to relax his back muscles, the tension aggravating his old injury.

"You okay?"

"Yeah, but I think I'm going to need a massage later."

Sandra's eyebrows bobbed up and down, a mischievous grin appearing. "Front, back, or both?"

Milton rolled his head toward her. "What the hell kind of question is that? Of course both!"

Sandra glanced at the stairs. "Race you to the bedroom."

Milton jumped to his feet, immediately regretting it as Sandra did the same. He reached forward and pushed her back on the couch, eliciting a surprised giggle.

The phone rang. "With Jim's timing, that'll be him." He pointed at her. "Don't think you're getting out of this, little lady." He grabbed the phone, pressing *Talk*. "Hello?"

"Hello, Señor Milton?"

His heart nearly stopped. The thick Spanish accent was unmistakable. It had to be bad news. "Yes."

"My name is Rosa Carona. I have a message from Laura Palmer."

Milton dropped back into his chair, grabbing the pen on the end table. "Yes?"

"She wants me to tell you that someone named Dylan knows what's going on. That he needs to be told that her husband and her friends are being held at El Jefe's compound in Tepich."

Milton wasn't sure what to say. "Wh-what's going on? I mean, who are you?"

"I can't talk long. Señora helped me escape. Now I repay her. You must send help or her husband and friends will die. Please, señor."

"Okay, I'll see what I can do. Is she with you?"

"No, she went after her husband."

Milton sighed as he closed his eyes, his head dropping back against his chair.

Why, Laura, why?

"Okay, I understand. And they are at this compound now?"

"Yes, they just arrived."

"Okay. Can I call you—"

The phone clicked, the dial tone sounding a moment later.

I guess not.

"What's wrong?"

"I'm not sure. I think Jim and Hugh have been kidnapped, and Laura is following them."

Sandra dropped onto the couch. "What! Who was that on the phone?"

"Some woman who claimed Laura saved her." He picked up his notes. "She said they were being held at El Jefe's compound in Tepich, and that Dylan apparently knows what's going on."

"Dylan Kane?"

"Yes."

"What are we going to do?"

Milton shook his head. "We need to get a message to Dylan, somehow."

"Call Washington?"

"Who in Washington? He's a spy. It's not like you can just call up Capitol Hill."

"Call the CIA."

"How the hell do you call a spy agency?"

Sandra tapped away at her eReader then handed it to him. "Go to their website and look up their number."

Milton stared at the screen, the contact number listed. "Holy shit!" He quickly dialed, the phone ringing before he even had a chance to think about what to say. It was answered by a human, not some machine.

"Hello, Dean Milton. How can I help you?"

His eyes popped wide as his heart slammed. "Umm, how did you know it was me?"

"We're the CIA."

That didn't make him feel any better about the situation. "Umm, I need to speak to Dylan Kane."

"I'm sorry, he's not available, but if you give me the message, I'll get it to him."

"Umm, who are you?"

"You can call me Chris."

"Umm, okay. Ahh, well, I just got a call from some woman named Rosa. Sorry, I didn't think to write down her last name. Actually, I'm not even sure if she mentioned it."

"Yes, go on."

Milton took a deep breath, trying to steady himself, his side of the conversation degenerating into babble. "Sorry. Listen, she says that Professor James Acton and others he was traveling with have been kidnapped."

"Yes, we're aware of the situation."

Milton paused. "Wait. What? You're aware?"

"Yes. You have information for us?"

"Well, I don't know. Maybe you already know."

"Why don't you tell me anyway?"

Milton exhaled, nodding. He wasn't thinking clearly, and was just wasting time. "Yes, you're right. Okay, this Rosa says that they are being held at El Jefe's compound in Tepich, and that Laura is following them."

There was a pause. "She said they were *held* there? As in they were already there?"

Milton tried to recall the conversation. "Yes. I definitely got the impression that they were there, not *going* to be there."

"And that's all she said?"

"Yes."

"Okay, thank you for calling us, goodbye."

"Wait!"

But it was too late, the line dead. He hung up and put the phone in its charger. He stared at his wife. "I think that was the scariest phone conversation I ever had."

"What do you mean?"

He stared at the phone. "I think we've got a direct line into the CIA."

Outskirts of Tepich, Mexico

Javier Diaz pushed through the trees, the sounds of life now filling his ears. He recognized a roof through the leaves and adjusted their course, the compound only a few hundred feet away. All he had to do was make it through those gates, and he'd be safe from whoever had been pursuing them.

Then he'd take fifty men and comb the entire area for them.

And when he got his hands on whoever was responsible, he'd slice them to pieces, slowly, letting them feel every cut of his blade as he stared into their eyes. Whoever had killed his men was already dead.

And so was their family.

And if it was one of Galano's men responsible, he'd personally castrate the prick and force-feed him his balls before slitting his throat.

He drew a long breath, the adrenaline surge at the thought of payback bringing a smile to his face.

Oh, yes, there will be blood.

He glanced at the hostages. Even if El Jefe kept them alive to collect the ransom, he'd see none of it. Perhaps a few whores as a reward, but little else. Were a few whores worth the death of four of his men? Four of his friends? In fact, El Jefe might even kill him for bringing them here, or for the loss of four good men.

Or you could collect the ransom yourself.

He paused, an unexpected debate raging. If he took the hostages, he could collect the ransom, and he'd be rich. He'd have enough money to get out of this shithole and free himself of the hold El Jefe had on him.

He continued forward, his lips pursed. Acton had promised them a million each in cash if they survived. But he had also agreed to ten million per hostage earlier.

Thirty million dollars.

All for him.

A sneer curled up the side of his face. He spun toward the last of his men and squeezed the trigger.

Nothing.

"Javier! What the hell!"

He stared at Ybanez for a moment as he battled with the jammed weapon, but Ybanez didn't stick around for answers. He sprinted back into the trees, disappearing into the dark. The weapon unjammed and he fired after him, spraying the entire area until his mag emptied.

Shit!

Laura froze as gunfire erupted ahead, the sounds of someone crashing through the jungle approaching. Her immediate thoughts were that her husband and the others were attempting an escape. This would be when they'd do it, probably desperate now that they were at the edge of the town. They had to know El Jefe's compound was close and that any hope of escape would die beyond the walls that apparently surrounded it. Yet she had to assume their plan had been an exchange for ransom.

If that were the case, then the end game would have had them going to the compound anyway.

Perhaps Rosa had been right.

Perhaps El Jefe would have killed them anyway, and they had found out and decided to make their escape.

She raised the AK-47 and aimed toward the trees in front of her, whoever had escaped now almost upon her. She lowered her aim, afraid she might panic and shoot an innocent. A man burst through the trees, his head turned behind him. In the dark, she couldn't tell who it was. Could it be James? Hugh? Eduardo?

"Hey!"

The man's head spun toward her, a shaft of moonlight illuminating his face. She squeezed the trigger and the man dropped without a sound. She rushed forward and kicked him over onto his back, confirming the brief glimpse she had caught had been right—this was a stranger.

Which meant there was only one left.

She charged forward as she reloaded, this perhaps the best chance she'd ever have of rescuing her husband and friends.

Someone crashing through the trees toward them made up Diaz's mind. Moments ago he was ready to go it alone, to cut El Jefe out completely and collect the ransom himself, but with a madman rushing their position, and the safety of the compound less than a hundred feet away, he had only one sure way to survive.

He grabbed the gringo and yanked him through the trees, quickly emerging onto the road that ran along the front of the compound. He sprinted toward the gate, the well-lit walls the most beautiful sight he had seen in days.

"Open the gate!" He spotted two lookouts as they aimed their weapons at them. "It's me, Javier! Open the gate!"

Somebody shouted the all-clear, and the hum of the motors kicked in, the gate rolling aside. He glanced over his shoulder and saw a shadow emerge from the woods, not a hundred paces from where he was.

Is that a woman?

He sprinted across the gate's track and into the safety of the compound, his hostages still behind him, their pursuer now out of sight. The gate rumbled closed and he spun toward the prisoners before any of his men could come within earshot.

"If any of you tell anyone what just happened, I'll make sure you die slow, painful deaths."

The gringo smiled at him slightly, the bastard knowing he now had leverage. "You just remember our deal. You keep us alive, and you get a million cash."

Diaz reasserted control "It was a million each. I want their shares too."

Acton opened his mouth to renegotiate, but Diaz cut him off with a gun pointed at the Mexican.

"Deal?"

Acton glared at him. "Deal."

Laura ducked back into the trees as Acton and the others disappeared into what must be El Jefe's compound. Rosa had described it as a fortress, and she was right. Built at the bottom of a hill, the property gently sloped upward, away from the road. A wall surrounded the entire complex—a well-lit wall topped with razor wire, a road ringing three sides. There was no way she was getting in there without being seen.

Her shoulders slumped. It was up to Rosa now. If she had made it home, would she have the courage to make the phone call? And if she had, was she even able to reach Greg? Greg might not even know they were missing, so might not think to answer a phone call at this hour, especially from a number he didn't recognize.

She sighed. And it might not matter even if he did. If Kane had never received her original message, then there would be no one here to help, regardless. If Milton were the first to know of their predicament, it could be days before anyone arrived to help them.

Her chest tightened as she stared at the compound, teeming no doubt with scores of heavily armed guards. It was hopeless.

Oh, James!

Operations Center 3, CIA Headquarters

Langley, Virginia

"Did we miss something?"

Shoulders were shrugged around the room, the phone conversation with James Acton's boss and friend, Gregory Milton, suggesting they had. Milton's number had been flagged in the system, with the computer tasked to send any calls he might make to a government facility, directly to Chris Leroux for the duration of this situation.

It had proven a wise move.

Though the result was confusing. The message from the survivor suggested they were already there, yet no one had been seen entering the compound since the convoy left.

"Sir, we've got movement."

Leroux turned, Sonya Tong pointing at the screen, a shot from the drone showing four people rushing through the gate. "Can we see their faces? Is that our people?"

Tong threw up her hands. "They're not doing anything with it! It's like the Mexicans haven't even noticed."

Leroux cursed then jabbed a finger toward the display. "Take over the drone. We need faces."

"Yes, sir." Tong's fingers flew over the keyboard, the drone banking hard to the left, the camera zooming in on the four new arrivals. "I have control."

Randy Child leaned forward in his chair. "Are those ropes?"

Leroux nodded, three of the arrivals clearly tied together. "I need faces."

"I'm trying, sir, but they're facing the wrong direction. I need to get the drone around for a better angle."

Leroux snapped his fingers, pointing at Child. "Get me Delta, now!"

North Side of Quintana Roo Cartel Compound

Tepich, Mexico

Command Sergeant Major Dawson brought the SUV to a halt on a road overlooking the compound, the walled estate poorly located from a strategic standpoint, the best place for it at the top of the hill, not the foot.

Though it probably didn't matter.

If the police were to ever raid the compound, it wouldn't matter where the compound was located—it would eventually fall. The defenses were designed around ensuring privacy and keeping rival gangs at bay, which with the numbers Langley was reporting inside, should be easy.

It was the departure of the convoy that had him interested, and as he scanned the scene below with his night vision goggles, he smiled at what he saw—or rather, didn't see. There were about a dozen guards outside, with an unknown number inside, though with it being a time of heightened tensions, he would assume El Jefe would have all hands on deck. And twelve outside wasn't enough to protect a compound that big.

The main gate rolled closed with a clang heard even from their position, suggesting it had been closed on an emergency setting. He could make out several figures, though only the top half of a couple of them, heads only for two others, the roofline of the house in the way. He was about to activate his comm when it squawked.

"Zero-One, Control. Come in, over."

"Control, Zero-One, we're in position north of the compound, over."

"Copy that, Zero-One. We believe the subjects have just arrived. We're showing four people just entering the compound's main entrance, now going inside the main structure."

Dawson cursed, slamming a fist into the steering wheel. If they had gone to the south, they would have run right into them before they even entered.

Timing is everything.

"Are you sure it's them?"

"Negative, but they came from the tree line."

Dawson exchanged annoyed glances with the others then paused. "Wait, did you say four?"

"Yes."

"Have you identified them yet?"

"No. We've got a bad angle from the UAV, but three are bound, all male."

Dawson's head bobbed as he resumed his surveillance. That fit with the intel. Sort of. Laura Palmer was believed to be following her husband and the others. If there were no women in this group, then that suggested she was either still free, or dead. He'd go under the former assumption for now, Palmer the toughest civilian woman he had ever met.

"We believe if she's still alive, she's in the immediate vicinity."

Niner poked his head between the seats. "Don't worry, my Laura is still alive and well and she's been kicking ass. There's no way only one man took Acton and Reading."

Dawson agreed. "What's the status of the Mexicans?"

"Mobilizing now. They'll be there in under fifteen minutes."

"And that convoy that left here?"

"Unknown. We'll have satellite coverage again in a few minutes, but we're almost positive they were heading for the police station. If they did arrive, it would take them a minimum of ten minutes to return. There's a large increase in cellphone traffic in the vicinity of the station, which suggests the attack has begun."

Dawson frowned. "Our contact, is he clear?"

"We haven't heard from him. He's turned off his phone, so we can't trace him either. What's your plan?"

Dawson scanned the area below, the defenses formidable, though nothing they hadn't handled before. "We're going in before the shit hits the fan."

"Wait a minute. Something's happening."

Everyone in the vehicle leaned to the left, staring through their goggles. Dawson spotted the problem.

Shit!

"Who the hell is that?"

Quintana Roo Cartel Compound
Tepich, Mexico

Javier Diaz headed for the main house, his multi-million dollar payday in tow. The portly Rayas emerged from inside and stared at the prisoners then at him with disgust.

"What the hell happened to you?"

Diaz glanced down at his clothing and realized he must be a sight. "Long story. Where the hell is everyone?"

"Gone to hit the police station and clean up your mess. Where the hell have you been?"

Diaz jerked a thumb at his prisoners. "Walking through the damned jungle for two days. Galano's men hit the lab and have been stalking us ever since. I lost five of my guys. Where are Daniel and Fernando? Did they make it back?"

Rayas shook his head. "No. Daniel is dead, and Fernando was arrested."

Diaz frowned.

That's not good.

"Did he talk?"

Rayas shrugged. "Dunno. El Jefe wants a complete cleanup, though." He gestured toward the hostages. "Who the hell are these guys?"

"Nosy neighbors. They claim to be rich."

"Huh. I don't think El Jefe's going to be happy. Too much heat right now."

And that means no payday.

"Where is he?"

"In his office." Rayas eyed the prisoners. "Want me to get something to tie them up a little better?"

Diaz glanced at the unbound hands of his prisoners, a necessary freedom in the jungle, an unwise one here. "Yeah, grab some zip ties for me." He yanked on the rope attached to the gringo as Rayas disappeared inside. "Let's go." He received a glare, but the three men followed him without complaint, Rayas rejoining them a few moments later, binding their hands. He knocked on El Jefe's closed office door.

"Come!"

Diaz opened the door and stepped inside.

"Javier!" El Jefe jumped from his seat and rounded his desk, giving him a thumping hug. "My old friend, I thought you were dead when I hadn't heard anything." He stepped back, curling up his nose. "You stink! What the hell happened?"

Diaz breathed a silent sigh of relief, half expecting a bullet to the head rather than a hug. "Galano's men hit the lab. When we went to pick up a stray, they sliced our tires and took our satphone. We've been walking through the jungle ever since." He lowered his chin and closed his eyes, trying to fake just the right amount of shame. "I lost five of my guys to them." He frowned, opening his eyes. "Six I guess. I wasn't aware of Daniel."

El Jefe flicked his wrist, dismissing the man as he returned to his chair. "He was killed by Officer Santana. We're dealing with him now." El Jefe turned his attention to the three prisoners. "And who are they?"

"Archaeologists or something. We found them nearby."

"Why didn't you just kill them?"

Diaz pointed to Acton. "This one claims they're rich. He's offered ten million dollars for each of their lives."

El Jefe's eyebrows climbed at the number, faint hope that he might see a payday returning to Diaz. "Thirty million dollars. Impressive." He regarded Morales. "*You* don't have ten million dollars." He stared at Acton. "You're the rich one, aren't you?"

Acton stepped forward. "Like I explained to your man, we all are."

"Bullshit." He jabbed a finger at Morales' left hand. "That's a twenty dollar watch. A rich man doesn't wear a twenty dollar watch." El Jefe leaned forward, glaring at Acton. "No bullshit. Who's got the money?"

Acton, remarkably, kept his cool. "I do." He stepped back, closer to his friends. "But if anything happens to them, then nobody gets any money."

El Jefe eyeballed him. "You think I need your money?"

"Everybody needs money."

El Jefe snorted. "You arrogant fool! You think just because I'm a Mexican means I'm automatically poor? That I don't know what rich is? I'm worth tens of millions. Hundreds! I employ hundreds in this town alone. I supply product to hundreds of thousands. And you know how?" He rose, leaning forward on his desk as he stared down Acton.

"By never showing mercy." He stood, holding out his hand to Diaz. "Gun."

Diaz's chest tightened as he handed over his Beretta. El Jefe stepped toward the prisoners, pointing the weapon at Morales. Acton stepped in front of the barrel. "You kill him, you get nothing."

El Jefe sneered at him. "Again, you have nothing I need." He pressed the muzzle against Acton's forehead. "I'm bored with this conversation."

En route to Quintana Roo Cartel Compound

Tepich, Mexico

Officer Hector Santana sat quietly in the back seat, squeezed between two of Galano's men as they raced toward El Jefe's compound, bringing up the rear of a large convoy of vehicles. The others were already talking about the attack on the police station, one of their informants in the community who lived near his place of work, phoning in with updates on the action.

I hope everybody stayed away.

Though if they did, the attack wouldn't take long, which would mean El Jefe's men could be back at any time. He closed his eyes, picturing Esperanza. The window was tight. Too tight. And El Jefe's home was a fortress with high walls and a heavy gate to keep them out. It could take them a long time just to get over the walls, by which time El Jefe's men could have returned.

No matter what, I have to get inside and rescue Esperanza.

To hell with the rest of them. He'd use them as a distraction. If they'd let him. He glanced sideways at the others.

There's no way they're letting you out of their sight.

The vehicle slowed, the compound just ahead. A pickup truck pulled up parallel to the gate and two men stood in the rear, rocket launchers on their shoulders. Two RPGs streaked toward the gate, the explosion ripping through the night, the aftermath felt by everyone. It was breathtaking. Another truck with what appeared to be a cowcatcher welded to the front, surged forward, shoving through the remains of the gate, leaving an opening for the rest of the vehicles.

He smiled slightly, impressed at how quickly Galano's men had gained entry. It meant hope for his Esperanza. But as the gunfire erupted, he realized the likelihood of her being killed in the crossfire was immense.

He leaned forward and Sanchez, Galano's number two man, turned to look at him. "Remember, if my wife dies, Galano doesn't get his tracker."

Sanchez laughed. "Who cares? If we kill El Jefe, we don't need it."

Santana's heart sank as he slumped back into his seat, the others laughing around him.

I'm sorry, Esperanza.

Quintana Roo Cartel Compound

Tepich, Mexico

Javier Diaz watched with a sinking heart as El Jefe's finger squeezed the trigger, the muzzle still pressed against his payday's forehead. An explosion rocked the house, shouts from the front followed by gunfire, causing everyone in the room to jump.

El Jefe lowered the weapon, turning toward Diaz. "What the hell was that?"

Diaz rushed to the window and peered outside. The gate was a smoldering wreck, and half a dozen vehicles were now inside the compound, spread out, scores of men pouring out of them, lead belching from their weapons. "Somebody's hitting the place!"

"Shit! Federales?"

Diaz shook his head, the vehicles and clothing not government. "No. Probably Galano's men."

"That sonofabitch! Call back our men. Now!" El Jefe strode toward the door as Diaz held out his hand, one of the men tossing him a phone.

"What about the hostages?"

"Kill them!"

Diaz followed El Jefe out of the office as he dialed, kicking himself for asking the question. If he had just kept his mouth shut, El Jefe might have forgotten about them and had time to rethink his decision.

He glanced at Rayas and jerked a thumb over his shoulder. "You heard him. Kill them."

Rayas drew his weapon and stepped back into the office. There was a cry then three shots rang out.

There goes three million bucks.

James Acton rushed to the door, peering out to see if they were about to have company. Leaving him with his hands bound by zip ties had been a mistake, a quick smack on the knees had broken them and allowed him to easily disarm the portly man sent to kill them. Three shots to his chest, with a one-second pause between each to suggest three different targets, would hopefully buy them enough time.

He grabbed a letter opener off the desk and freed the other's hands, then they all worked at the knots to the rope looping them together at the waist. "We need to get the hell out of here."

Reading agreed. "No argument here."

Acton checked their would-be killer for ammo, finding a single magazine. "We'll get more weapons as we go." Footfalls echoed in the hallway. He eyed the door then looked about. "We can't leave him here." He pointed at a side door. "Check it out."

Morales stepped over and carefully opened the door. "Empty."

"Help me."

Reading grabbed an arm and they pulled the body through the side door, the only light the flash of gunfire and explosions from the front.

Somebody whimpered.

Acton dropped the body, spinning toward the sound as he reached for the weapon stuffed in his belt. Morales found a light switch and flicked it on, revealing a terrified woman bound and gagged in the corner.

Acton lowered his weapon and rushed over. He removed the gag and worked on the ropes. "Are you okay?" he asked in Spanish.

The woman nodded, though her eyes suggested she wasn't sure. "Y-yes."

"Who are you?"

"Esperanza Santana. I'm a prisoner like you, I guess."

Acton cut through the rope binding her hands. "Why are they holding you?"

"I'm the wife of a police officer. I think they want my husband to come." Her eyes widened slightly, looking toward the window. "Is that him? Maybe the police are here!"

Morales peered out the window and shook his head. "No, civilian vehicles and no uniforms. Looks like another gang."

She frowned. "Probably Galano's men." She spat on the floor as Acton freed her legs and helped her to her feet.

"Can you walk?"

She took several tentative steps. "Yes."

"Do you know how to get out of here?"

She shook her head. "No. I've never been here before."

Several bullets tore through the window Morales was standing by, burying themselves into the opposite wall.

"We've gotta get out of here," said Reading.

Acton agreed, stepping toward the door leading to El Jefe's office. "Let's get to the rear of the building. Maybe we can find a way out there." He held out his hand for Esperanza. She hesitated. "Trust me. You don't want to be here when this is over, no matter who wins. Not as a cop's wife."

She trembled then rushed toward him, grabbing his hand. "Thank you."

South Side of Quintana Roo Cartel Compound

Tepich, Mexico

Laura sprinted through the trees at a crouch, praying she didn't get struck by a stray bullet, far too many of the defenders' rounds fired blindly. Defenders who appeared to be losing. These weren't police hitting the compound, which meant it wasn't help from Kane—unless he was working with local criminals now. And criminals with this much firepower were definitely into dealing drugs, and despite the CIAs ignominious history, she couldn't see Kane working with them. No, this was something else. Perhaps the same people who hit the drug lab were now hitting El Jefe's compound. It made sense. This was an all-out war between two drug gangs.

And her husband and friends were caught in the crossfire.

She had to figure out a way inside before it was too late. The gang attacking the compound was likely there to kill everyone. They wouldn't care about hostages, in fact, they wouldn't even know there *were* hostages. They'd simply enter the room where they were held, and spray them with bullets.

And should they manage to survive the assault, these new arrivals might take them as hostages of their own, and with no vehicle, she'd have no way of following them. Her beloved would be lost to her forever.

And she couldn't let that happen.

North Side of Quintana Roo Cartel Compound
Tepich, Mexico

Command Sergeant Major Dawson watched the fight unfold, the defenders clearly outnumbered, though because of their defensive positions, they were holding the line, the attackers not making it out of the front courtyard. A lot were dying, which suited him just fine. If every drug dealer dropped dead tomorrow, the world would be a better place. If they dropped dead right now, it would make his life much simpler.

Unfortunately, that wasn't likely to happen. Though waiting was an option, the longer they did, the more chance there was of Acton and the others being killed in the crossfire, or simply executed to eliminate a headache El Jefe didn't have time to deal with right now.

"Zero-One, Control. We've got targets exiting the rear of the main building. Looks like four."

Dawson peered through the goggles, spotting the targets. "Are they our people?"

"Standby, we don't have the angle."

Niner's voice came over the comm, he and Atlas positioned nearby with a sniper rifle. "This is One-One, I've got no joy here. There's a row of trees in the way, over."

Dawson leaned out the window of their SUV, hoping the extra few inches might let him get a clearer look at the faces, but it was no use, the same trees blocking Niner's view fulfilling their task—privacy from prying eyes.

A frustrated Niner squawked in his ear. "They're getting in a vehicle. I've got a shot, but I don't know who they are, over."

"Hold your fire, One-One." He glanced at Spock, shaking his head, the operator's frustration clear. "We've gotta know now, Control."

"Stand by."

Dawson put the vehicle in gear.

"Negative, Zero-One. They're not our targets. Facial recognition shows it is El Jefe and three unsubs, probably just his people."

"Copy that, Control." Dawson watched as the much smaller rear gate opened.

While we're here…

"Permission to take them out."

"Negative, Zero-One. Not the objective. Leave them to the Mexicans."

The SUV's tires spun, a cloud of dust forming as the truck sped toward the gate. As it cleared, muzzle flashes from half a dozen weapons sliced through the night, whoever was attacking having the forethought to pre-position men to cover the rear. The SUV skidded to a halt as the six men advanced, continuing to pour lead on the armored vehicle. The front windshield finally gave, and within moments, the guns stopped.

"Umm, Langley, I don't think we'll be worrying about El Jefe anymore."

"Copy that, Zero-One. No tears shed here."

Quintana Roo Cartel Compound

Tepich, Mexico

Officer Hector Santana ducked behind a massive fountain that occupied the center of the courtyard, choosing his shots carefully, knowing he'd never be able to live with himself if it were his own stray bullet that killed his beloved Esperanza. The battle was at a near standstill, and if it weren't won soon, he had no doubt those sent to hit the police station would return shortly, cutting off their escape.

He had to act now and get Esperanza before that happened. But how? He searched for an opening, any opening, yet found none. The defenders had the front of the house covered.

Or did they?

He watched where the muzzle flashes were coming from, and they all were from the roof over the main entrance, or the windows clustered around it. The house was long and narrow, with the front an impressive inverted V shape. Almost all of the defenders were clustered around the main entrance at the tip of the V, leaving the outer edges exposed. From what he could see, there were no defenders there at all. If he could just reach the side of the house, he might escape their field of fire.

Though he was just as likely to get killed in the process.

James Acton peered through the doorway leading to the outside, the smoking remains of an SUV visible through the open gate. And six armed men, slowly entering. "Can't go that way."

Reading cursed. "Bloody hell. We can't go out the front, can't go out the back."

Morales pointed down a long hallway to their left. "Sides?"

Acton stared down the vacant hall. "I don't see that we have much choice." He took point as they rushed down the hallway, the entire outer wall made of glass, the only thing not making them painfully visible was the fact the lights were out, either the power intentionally cut by someone, or the lines taken out in the gunfight.

Two armed men stepped out in front of him and Acton raised his weapon as they lowered their jaws. Double taps took them both out, Acton not slowing his stride an iota. "Let's move. Somebody probably heard that."

Laura made her way back down the side of the compound, the rear entrance a no go, another smaller yet still significant gun battle occurring there as well. She eyed the wall, easily ten feet tall with razor wire across the top.

How the hell am I getting over that?

She searched about for an option, any option, her eyes settling on an idling box van, stopped at an angle, its owner perhaps fleeing the gunfire, the road it was on winding around the compound, there no options but to pass the front or rear entrance. She didn't blame the driver. She probably would have done the same.

She jumped in and put it in gear, hammering on the gas as she raced down the side of the compound, then slammed on the brakes before she became visible to those at the front entrance. She turned around then took a quick breath.

This is colossally daft.

She floored it, gripping the steering wheel tight, her AK-47 resting on her lap, her Beretta tucked into her belt.

And prayed.

James Acton opened the door, the security panel chirping in protest, obviously on backup battery power. "Well, someone knows we're here." He peered outside, finding no one in sight, the compound much darker than when they had arrived. "Okay, the wall's about thirty feet from here, and it looks like we're clear."

Reading poked his head out. "How the hell are we getting over that?"

Acton looked back at the wall. Reading was right. They might be able to boost each other to the top if it weren't for the fact there was razor wire running along it, and if he knew his drug lords, probably shards of jagged glass embedded in the concrete. "We need to find something to climb it with. A rope, a ladder, anything." Acton spotted a shed near the rear corner. "That looks like some sort of gardener's shed. There might be a ladder in there. You guys stay here, I'll go get it."

Reading grabbed him by the shoulder. "No, I'll go. I'm the cop."

Acton smiled. "Yeah, and I'm a decade younger." He nodded toward the gun Reading had taken off one of the men Acton had just killed. "You watch them. I'll be back."

Reading wasn't happy, but nodded then grabbed him by the arm. "Don't you go getting yourself killed just so you can join Laura."

Acton stared him in the eyes as he struggled to maintain control at the mention of his late wife's name. "I'll be back."

Officer Santana sprinted toward a large planter to his left, blasting at the nearest enemy position, providing his own cover fire, his shout of "cover me" apparently falling on deaf ears. He dove, rolling behind the slab of formed concrete as the interlocking brick drive was torn up behind him. He uprighted himself then rushed toward the half height wall of the terrace that ran along the front of the house, leaping over the edge and hitting the tile hard.

I'm getting too old for this.

He didn't care what happened today, though if he survived, he was retiring. Mexico was going to hell, all so the gringos could have their drugs. There was just too much money in it, and the country was still too poor, despite the influx of jobs over the past two decades. Cops like him were paid poorly, which made bribes simply too tempting. Americans couldn't understand how things were down here. If their police were paid the same as a burger flipper at McDonald's, and shot at every day, would they be surprised when their police took bribes to help stop the bullets coming their way and supplement their meager salary?

Yet that was how it was here. If a cop stood up to the gangs, they were killed. If a cop didn't, and instead kept his eyes shut to what was happening, he might survive, though would still live a pretty poor existence on his government salary. But on the take? It meant safety, women, booze, drugs, and any other vice one might have. It meant a better life than any cop could ever hope to have. He had always been able to resist, though too often he had looked the other way.

And tonight that was over. No matter what happened, the two biggest gangs in town were here, killing each other, and the Federales were already staging nearby. They'd catch wind of this, he was certain, and would be here soon to clean up this mess. All he cared about now was his wife.

God, please, just keep my Esperanza safe.

Laura cranked the wheel to the right, shoving the gas pedal to the floor as she braced herself. The impact with the compound wall was jarring. Her head shot forward and slammed into the steering wheel, there no airbags in this beast. She was dazed for a moment, a loud blinding sound ringing through her head as she regained focus.

She opened her eyes and smiled, a large hole in the wall. She pushed the door but it was blocked, the truck straddling what was left of the wall, the doors wedged shut.

Shit.

The windshield was a shattered mess of safety glass. She smacked at it with the butt of her AK-47 and it splintered away, finally falling free. She climbed out onto the hood and dropped to the ground, crouching as she scanned the area. A massive gun battle was happening to her right at the front gate, just out of sight. The rear was now nearly silent, only sporadic fire. No one was in sight, but there was no way her handiwork hadn't been heard by somebody.

She caught her breath as a dark figure emerged from a shed to her left, carrying something.

Is that a ladder?

Something moved ahead of her, a figure in an open doorway. She held her fire, not wanting to give away her position and not clear on who she'd be shooting at. She spotted the outline of a gun gripped in the shadow's hand, and raised her weapon.

But hesitated.

Without changing her aim, she glanced to her left at the man frozen in place, now certain it was a ladder gripped in his hand.

A ladder gripped by the man she loved.

"James!"

James Acton stood frozen in place. The hood of a truck was visible, a large hole now in the wall they were about to climb. There was no way this was an accident, and his immediate instinct was to run, a third front about to be opened up, this side of the compound undefended for the moment. A figure climbed through the windshield and crawled across the hood, silhouetted in the darkness. A weapon aimed toward the door where Reading and the others stood. He was about to shout a warning when he heard his name.

And he would recognize that voice anywhere.

His jaw dropped as his shoulders slumped, everything forgotten as the ladder clattered at his side. She was alive. The love of his life was alive. It had been her all along that had followed them, that had killed five of their kidnappers, and was here now, rescuing them.

"Laura!" He sprinted toward her when something caught his eye. Someone was on the roof. Gunfire tore at the wall beside him and he dove to the ground, but not before something tore at his leg.

"James!"

Laura watched in horror as her husband was hit. She spun toward the source of the gunfire, spotting two men on the roof, and opened fire, the first dropping, the second taking cover. She heard shouts, the words not understood though their meaning clear from the tone.

Help was being called for.

There were shouts from the front gate, some sounding like cheers, quickly followed by a massive increase in firepower.

Something's changed.

"Taking the shot." Niner squeezed the trigger and the target dropped. He adjusted his aim so he could check on Acton and sighed with relief as he saw the toughest civilian he had ever met, push to his feet.

"Wait, three more targets headed toward them."

Niner adjusted his aim, Atlas playing spotter today.

"Hold, they're friendlies. Looks like we've got the two professors, Agent Reading, our Mexican professor, and one civilian female."

Niner's eyebrows rose. "Don't tell me Reading picked up another chick in the jungle."

Atlas grunted. "Chicks dig the British accent."

Niner debated attempting one, deciding against it, already knowing his was terrible. "What aboot Sco-ish?"

Atlas eyeballed him. "You're going to die a lonely old man. In fact, I don't think you've ever known the touch of a woman."

Niner opened his mouth for a witty retort when Atlas cut him off. "Wait, we've got more company. Shit, they just went out of sight."

Niner scanned the compound. "Where?"

"Approaching the one-two corner. Opposite side of the building."

Niner adjusted his aim but could see no one from their position. "Zero-One, we've got hostiles approaching their position and no shot. One-Two corner, over."

"On it. Stand by."

Officer Santana stared over his shoulder, panic setting in. El Jefe's men had returned, the odds switching back to the crime lord's favor, Galano's men now fighting on two fronts, quickly getting mowed down. He spotted three fleeing toward the side of the house he was heading for, and hit the deck, the half wall hiding his position as they sprinted by. They rounded the corner and he heard shouts. Someone screamed. And it was a voice he recognized.

"Esperanza!"

Laura spun, raising her AK-47 as the woman with Reading screamed and pointed. Laura squeezed the trigger, not hesitating to fire, everyone she knew already within sight. Two of the men dropped as the bumper of the truck bounced. Gunfire erupted behind her and she dropped, spinning backward as she turned to take aim at the new arrival. "BD!"

Dawson hopped to the ground, Spock following him as they quickly advanced toward the corner, the new arrivals dead. They fell back toward the hole she had made, and she sighed with relief.

"You got my message!"

Dawson gave her a quick two-fingered salute. "Yup, Dylan was able to get things rolling. Now let's get the hell out of here."

The thunder of chopper blades in the distance could be heard and felt, even more relief sweeping through her. Helicopters meant government, which meant they'd be safe soon. Dawson killed those thoughts.

"The Federales are going to be here any second now with orders to kill everything."

Her chest tightened. Had they gone through all of this just to be killed in the end by the good guys? Dawson pointed to Acton. "You good to move?"

He nodded. "Just a scratch."

Reading grabbed him, tossed Acton's arm over his shoulder, then helped him toward the truck.

Dawson activated his comm. "One-One, come get us." Dawson climbed up on the hood, pulling Laura up then the Mexican woman.

"Esperanza!"

They all spun toward the voice, Laura raising her weapon as the woman cried out. "Hector!"

Dawson slapped Laura's weapon down. "Hold your fire, friendly!" The man rushed toward the woman, hugging her hard. "Let's go, now!" shouted Dawson.

Laura helped pull Acton onto the hood, Reading pushing from behind as Dawson rushed toward the reunited couple, urging them to save the hugs for later. "Let's go, Santana. No time for that!"

So he knows him.

She helped James over the top of the truck then leaped to the ground, Reading flipping over the back with a grunt. He held up his hands and helped Acton down, Morales following a moment later, then the Mexican woman and Santana, whom Laura assumed was her husband from the way they had kissed.

A massive explosion at the front of the compound signaled the arrival of someone with heavy ordnance. Dawson hopped to the ground, Spock following as an SUV raced toward them. Laura raised her weapon when Dawson put a hand on the barrel, gently lowering it. It skidded to a halt feet away, the window down. Niner leaned out.

"Somebody order an Uber?"

James Acton climbed into the back seat, pushing all the way to the far side, Laura following him. He grabbed her and held her tight, his eyes squeezed shut. He never wanted to let her go. He had been certain she was dead, there simply no reason to believe it was her following them.

There had been a signal from the tracking device Diaz's men had been carrying, so someone else had been out there.

Maybe they were with her.

But she was alone now. He had a million questions, yet they could wait. They'd *have* to wait.

"I thought you were dead."

She gazed up at him, smiling. "You should know by now that I have nine lives."

He chuckled. "How many did you use up this time?"

She shrugged. "I'm afraid to count. At least you were the one that got shot this time." She pressed gently on the tear in his pants and he winced. "You okay?"

He nodded. "It only hurts if someone touches it."

Her hand darted away. "Sorry."

He laughed. "Forget about it."

The final door slammed shut, everyone crammed inside.

"Let's get the hell out of here!" shouted Dawson from the passenger seat. Niner hammered on the gas and cranked the wheel, the back end spinning out as they pulled a 180, sending them hurtling toward the rear of the compound. Dawson activated his comm as Acton stared out the window, helicopters circling the area, a large gun battle to their right. "Control, Zero-One. Advise the Mexicans that they've got friendlies on the road to the north side of the compound in a black SUV. We've rescued all the hostages, over."

Everyone sat in silence, waiting for some indication from Dawson that the message had been received. A helicopter roared overhead, a beam of light slicing through the night sky, lighting them up like they were delivering a soliloquy on Broadway. Another chopper raced toward them, its posture aggressive.

"He's about to open fire, BD!" shouted Niner as he kept the accelerator floored.

"Control, if you don't call them off now, we're dead!"

Acton gripped Laura tight, trying to ignore what was about to happen. He had his Laura back, and if they were to die now, at least they would die together. The chopper banked hard to the right, breaking off its attack run and Niner whooped, punching the roof several times.

"Talk about timing!"

Dawson gave a thumbs up. "Langley confirms the Federales have cleared us." He leaned out the window and waved at the chopper still highlighting them, the light turning off a moment later. "Let's head to the staging area." Dawson turned around so he could look at them. "We've got a plane waiting for you. You'll be home soon."

Laura leaned forward. "We've got one stop to make first."

Dawson stared at her. "Excuse me?"

"Did you get a message from a Rosa Carona?"

He nodded. "Yeah, Langley said they got an update passed through Dean Milton. Thanks to her we knew where to look, or more accurately, when."

Laura smiled.

Good girl.

She turned to Santana. "Do you know where Rosa Carona lives?"

"Yes. Why?"

"I promised to get her and her family out of here."

Dawson cleared his throat. "Can't that wait?"

She shook her head. "No, if it weren't for her, we might all be dead right now."

Dawson looked at Santana and jerked a thumb at Niner. "Tell the man where to go."

Rosa Carona Residence
Tepich, Mexico

Rosa sat in the dark, huddled with her husband and their kids, trembling at the sounds of a major battle not far enough away. The horizon flashed with each explosion, helicopters roaring overhead as sirens blared in the distance. The Federales had arrived, and by the sounds of it, were finally hitting El Jefe's compound.

I hope he dies.

But it meant she no longer had a job, and if he survived, it meant she was dead. She was the last survivor. And there was no way they'd leave her alive.

A vehicle coming to a rapid halt outside had her heart hammering. There was a firm knock on the door and the children cried out in terror.

"Rosa, it's me, Laura!"

She breathed a sigh of relief and leaped to her feet, rushing toward the door. She yanked it open and cried out, hugging this stranger whom she barely knew.

"You made it. Your husband? Is he okay?"

Laura pointed toward the vehicle, a second one pulling up behind them. "Yes. Are you ready?"

Tears filled Rosa's eyes. "You're keeping your promise?"

Laura smiled. "Of course. Let's just get you someplace safe first, then you decide where you want to go."

Rosa collapsed in her arms and tightly hugged this strange, terrifying woman.

Thank you, God.

Universidad Veracruzana Archaeological Site
South of Tepich, Mexico

James Acton frowned at the necessary sight. A dozen armed guards patrolled the perimeter of the archaeological site, now appearing to be more of an armed camp than a place of learning. Yet they had no choice. This was too important a find to ignore, but the area was too dangerous to have students work in, unprotected.

He descended the stairs to the chambers, and a student rushed by, bumping into his leg. He winced.

"Sorry, señor."

Acton dismissed the apology with a wave. "No worries." His leg was still a little tender from where he had been grazed, but he was in good shape considering. He stepped into the second chamber, finding Laura pouring over the texts, helping Morales translate, more excited than he had seen her in a long time. Reading sat in a chair nearby, sipping a beer.

"Where the hell did you find that?"

He shrugged. "I'm on vacation and surrounded by students."

Acton chuckled, a new batch of students arriving this morning after the government provided security team had given the all-clear. Laura's team was on its way to provide supplementary security until things settled down, which could be days, possibly weeks or worse.

The carnage at the compound had been unreal. Well over one hundred dead. El Jefe was dead, as were most of his men. Galano's men were slaughtered as well, and he had been arrested, though escaped custody within less than 24 hours, several guards believed to have been bribed to look the other way. He was at large, and Acton had little doubt he'd remain that way.

The tracker Officer Santana had found had been used to shut down all of El Jefe's drug labs, and it wouldn't make a dent in the supply, the void left behind probably already filled by those that remained. Delta had left the same night, on to whatever their next mission was. Santana and his wife had relocated to where their children were in Mexico City, and Rosa and her family were settling in with relatives in the northeast, about as far from here as she could possibly get, Laura having set her up with enough money to give them a fresh start, but not ruin their lives with a sudden windfall.

So many were dead, so many innocents. And they had almost become part of the statistic. Laura caught him staring at her and smiled. He winked.

Reading put down his beer. "That's one hell of a woman you've got there."

Acton smiled. "Tell me about it. She saved us all. If it weren't for her, we'd be dead."

"Yup. There but for the grace of God…"

Laura gasped, her hand darting to her mouth.

"What is it?" Concerned, Acton headed toward his wife, Reading struggling out of his chair to follow.

She pointed at the table. "This. The last parchment."

"What about it?"

"It's about what happened to the messenger who warned them about the Chinese."

Acton's eyes narrowed. "What? What happened?"

Laura stared up at him, her eyes filled with tears, then her head fell into his chest.

Chichen Itza, Maya Empire
1092 AD

"Nelli!" Balam Canek cried out the name of the woman he loved as he watched her head tumble down the stone steps of the massive temple, her lifeless body yanked away from the sacrificial altar and tossed over the edge into a pile of bodies below.

Tears rolled down his cheeks as his vision blurred, his heart hammering hard, blood roaring in his ears. It was all his fault. He should never have allowed her to come with him.

He had been selfish.

Perhaps this was his punishment for betraying tradition. A chief was supposed to cast off his former life and start anew for the good of his community, as was the will of the gods. He had defied tradition, defied the will of the gods, and though they continued to bless their subjects with a steady rain, it was clear his blood was also part of their desire.

And their wrath.

He felt a hand in his, squeezing it tightly. He stared down at the blue hand, then up at his enemy's face, the sorrow of the loss of Nelli written in his former enemy's eyes.

They were equals now. No longer opposing warriors, no longer enemies. They were both painted in blue, they were the property of the gods, and their moments left on this earth were few.

"I'm sorry I brought you here."

And he meant it. Faced with his impending death, he realized they were all men, they were all equal, no matter where they had come from, or what god they served. In the end, they were the same. They lived, they loved, and they died.

He wiped his eyes clear and stared down the steps at the head of his beloved, and his chest heaved in agony. The priest motioned at him, and the acolytes grabbed him by the arms, dragging him toward the altar as the crowds below roared their approval. His head was shoved forward, ropes draped over his back and tightened, forcing him flat on the slab of stone, cold and wet from blood.

He forced his eyes open, twisting his head so he could see Nelli, her dead eyes staring up at him.

"I'll be with you soon, my love."

The priest ended his prayer.

And the executioner grunted.

THE END

ACKNOWLEDGEMENTS

The idea for this book came from two different sources. One was from reading years ago about the belief the Chinese had actually visited the Americas long before Columbus, and the other was from reading about the fall of the Mayan Empire. The drought depicted in this book actually did happen, and it did end at some point, though not before irreparably harming the Mayan civilization. The arrival of the Spanish ultimately sealed their fate. The burning of much of their culture, and the pillaging of their treasures, destroyed most hope of ever truly understanding these people.

That was the history portion of the book, and I loved writing it. For the modern day, with the book having to take place geographically where the Mayans were historically, I was able to have a new villain I hadn't employed before. No cults, no governments, no terrorists, just straight up greedy criminals. Researching this aspect of things, and reading about the violence involved in the drug trade, was an eye-opener, and this book is dedicated to the victims. I fear tens of thousands, if not more, will die before this is over, if it ever is.

Now here's a little trivia item for you. In the book, I make reference to flat foreheads on the Mayans. This is actually a thing! Skeletal remains have found this deformity on far too many skulls for it to not have been commonplace. The theory is that boards were strapped to the heads of babies, when the skull is still soft, reforming the forehead over time.

Crazy stuff, though I guess no different than the binding of feet that was common practice in China.

As usual, there are people to thank, though not as many as usual. My father, of course, for all the research, Brent Richards for some military equipment info, Fred Newton for some nautical terminology info, Susan "Miss Boss" Turnbull for a last minute save, and my proofreading team. And, as usual, my wife, daughter, and mother.

To those who have not already done so, please visit my website at www.jrobertkennedy.com then sign up for the Insider's Club to be notified of new book releases. Your email address will never be shared or sold, and you'll only receive the occasional email from me as I don't have time to spam you!

Thank you once again for reading.

ABOUT THE AUTHOR

With over 650,000 books in circulation and over 3000 five-star reviews, USA Today bestselling author J. Robert Kennedy has been ranked by Amazon as the #1 Bestselling Action Adventure novelist based upon combined sales. He is the author of over thirty international bestsellers including the smash hit James Acton Thrillers. He lives with his wife and daughter and writes full-time.

Visit Robert's website at www.jrobertkennedy.com for the latest news and contact information, and to join the Insider's Club to be notified when new books are released.

J. ROBERT KENNEDY

Available James Acton Thrillers

The Protocol (Book #1)

For two thousand years, the Triarii have protected us, influencing history from the crusades to the discovery of America. Descendent from the Roman Empire, they pervade every level of society, and are now in a race with our own government to retrieve an ancient artifact thought to have been lost forever.

Brass Monkey (Book #2)

A nuclear missile, lost during the Cold War, is now in play--the most public spy swap in history, with a gorgeous agent the center of international attention, triggers the end-game of a corrupt Soviet Colonel's twenty five year plan. Pursued across the globe by the Russian authorities, including a brutal Spetsnaz unit, those involved will stop at nothing to deliver their weapon, and ensure their payday, regardless of the terrifying consequences.

Broken Dove (Book #3)

With the Triarii in control of the Roman Catholic Church, an organization founded by Saint Peter himself takes action, murdering one of the new Pope's operatives. Detective Chaney, called in by the Pope to investigate, disappears, and, to the horror of the Papal staff sent to inform His Holiness, they find him missing too, the only clue a secret chest, presented to each new pope on the eve of their election, since the beginning of the Church.

The Templar's Relic (Book #4)

The Vault must be sealed, but a construction accident leads to a miraculous discovery--an ancient tomb containing four Templar Knights, long forgotten, on the grounds of the Vatican. Not knowing who they can trust, the Vatican requests Professors James Acton and Laura Palmer examine the find, but what they discover, a precious Islamic relic, lost during the Crusades, triggers a set of events that shake the entire world, pitting the two greatest religions against each other. At risk is nothing less than the Vatican itself, and the rock upon which it was built.

Flags of Sin (Book #5)

Archaeology Professor James Acton simply wants to get away from everything, and relax. A trip to China seems just the answer, and he and his fiancée, Professor Laura Palmer, are soon on a flight to Beijing. But while boarding, they bump into an old friend, Delta Force Command Sergeant Major Burt Dawson, who surreptitiously delivers a message that they must meet the next day, for Dawson knows something they don't. China is about to erupt into chaos.

The Arab Fall (Book #6)

An accidental find by a friend of Professor James Acton may lead to the greatest archaeological discovery since the tomb of King Tutankhamen, perhaps even greater. And when news of it spreads, it reaches the ears of a group hell-bent on the destruction of all idols and icons, their mere existence considered blasphemous to Islam.

The Circle of Eight (Book #7)

The Bravo Team is targeted by a madman after one of their own intervenes in a rape. Little do they know this internationally well-respected banker is also a senior member of an organization long thought extinct, whose stated goals for a reshaped world are not only terrifying, but with today's globalization, totally achievable.

The Venice Code (Book #8)

A former President's son is kidnapped in a brazen attack on the streets of Potomac by the very ancient organization that murdered his father, convinced he knows the location of an item stolen from them by the late president. A close friend awakes from a coma with a message for archaeology Professor James Acton from the same organization, sending him on a quest to find an object only rumored to exist, while trying desperately to keep one step ahead of a foe hell-bent on possessing it.

Pompeii's Ghosts (Book #9)
Two thousand years ago Roman Emperor Vespasian tries to preserve an empire by hiding a massive treasure in the quiet town of Pompeii should someone challenge his throne. Unbeknownst to him nature is about to unleash its wrath upon the Empire during which the best and worst of Rome's citizens will be revealed during a time when duty and honor were more than words, they were ideals worth dying for.

Amazon Burning (Book #10)
Days from any form of modern civilization, archaeology Professor James Acton awakes to gunshots. Finding his wife missing, taken by a member of one of the uncontacted tribes, he and his friend INTERPOL Special Agent Hugh Reading try desperately to find her in the dark of the jungle, but quickly realize there is no hope without help. And with help three days away, he knows the longer they wait, the farther away she'll be.

The Riddle (Book #11)
Russia accuses the United States of assassinating their Prime Minister in Hanoi, naming Delta Force member Sergeant Carl "Niner" Sung as the assassin. Professors James Acton and Laura Palmer, witnesses to the murder, know the truth, and as the Russians and Vietnamese attempt to use the situation to their advantage on the international stage, the husband and wife duo attempt to find proof that their friend is innocent.

Blood Relics (Book #12)
A DYING MAN. A DESPERATE SON.
ONLY A MIRACLE CAN SAVE THEM BOTH.
Professor Laura Palmer is shot and kidnapped in front of her husband, archaeology Professor James Acton, as they try to prevent the theft of the world's Blood Relics, ancient artifacts thought to contain the blood of Christ, a madman determined to possess them all at any cost.

Sins of the Titanic (Book #13)

THE ASSEMBLY IS ETERNAL. AND THEY'LL STOP AT NOTHING TO KEEP IT THAT WAY.

When Professor James Acton is contacted about a painting thought to have been lost with the sinking of the Titanic, he is inadvertently drawn into a century old conspiracy an ancient organization known as The Assembly will stop at nothing to keep secret.

Saint Peter's Soldiers (Book #14)

A MISSING DA VINCI.
A TERRIFYING GENETIC BREAKTHROUGH.
A PAST AND FUTURE ABOUT TO COLLIDE!

In World War Two a fabled da Vinci drawing is hidden from the Nazis, those involved fearing Hitler may attempt to steal it for its purported magical powers. It isn't returned for over fifty years. And today, archaeology Professor James Acton and his wife are about to be dragged into the terrible truth of what happened so many years ago, for the truth is never what it seems, and the history we thought was fact, is all lies.

The Thirteenth Legion (Book #15)

A TWO-THOUSAND-YEAR-OLD DESTINY IS ABOUT TO BE FULFILLED!

USA Today bestselling author J. Robert Kennedy delivers another action-packed thriller in The Thirteenth Legion. After Interpol Agent Hugh Reading spots his missing partner in Berlin, it sets off a chain of events that could lead to the death of his best friends, and if the legends are true, life as we know it.

Raging Sun (Book #16)

WILL A SEVENTY-YEAR-OLD MATTER OF HONOR TRIGGER THE NEXT GREAT WAR?

The Imperial Regalia have been missing since the end of World War Two, and the Japanese government, along with the new—and secretly illegitimate—emperor, have been lying to the people. But the truth isn't out yet, and the Japanese will stop at nothing to secure their secret and retrieve the ancient relics confiscated by a belligerent Russian government. Including war.

Wages of Sin (Book #17)
WHEN IS THE PRICE TO PROTECT A NATION'S LEGACY TOO HIGH?

Jim and Laura are on safari in South Africa when a chance encounter leads to a clue that could unlock the greatest mystery remaining of the Boer War over a century ago—the location to over half a billion dollars in gold!

Wrath of the Gods (Book #18)
A THOUSAND YEARS OF HISTORY ARE ABOUT TO BE REWRITTEN!

A strange people land on the shores of the Mayan Empire, triggering a battle for the very survival of a civilization already in upheaval. A thousand years later, Acton and Laura are invited to an incredible discovery that reveals the truth of what happened, yet before they can fully explore this amazing find, they are thrust into the middle of the Mexican drug war.

Available Special Agent Dylan Kane Thrillers

Rogue Operator (Book #1)
Three top secret research scientists are presumed dead in a boating accident, but the kidnapping of their families the same day raises questions the FBI and local police can't answer, leaving them waiting for a ransom demand that will never come. Central Intelligence Agency Analyst Chris Leroux stumbles upon the story, finding a phone conversation that was never supposed to happen, and is told to leave it to the FBI. But he can't let it go. For he knows something the FBI doesn't. One of the scientists is alive.

Containment Failure (Book #2)
New Orleans has been quarantined, an unknown virus sweeping the city, killing one hundred percent of those infected. The Centers for Disease Control, desperate to find a cure, is approached by BioDyne Pharma who reveal a former employee has turned a cutting edge medical treatment capable of targeting specific genetic sequences into a weapon, and released it. The stakes have never been higher as Kane battles to save not only his friends and the country he loves, but all of mankind.

Cold Warriors (Book #3)

While in Chechnya CIA Special Agent Dylan Kane stumbles upon a meeting between a known Chechen drug lord and a retired General once responsible for the entire Soviet nuclear arsenal. Money is exchanged for a data stick and the resulting transmission begins a race across the globe to discover just what was sold, the only clue a reference to a top-secret Soviet weapon called Crimson Rush.

Death to America (Book #4)

America is in crisis. Dozens of terrorist attacks have killed or injured thousands, and worse, every single attack appears to have been committed by an American citizen in the name of Islam. A stolen experimental F-35 Lightning II is discovered by CIA Special Agent Dylan Kane in China, delivered by an American soldier reported dead years ago in exchange for a chilling promise. And Chris Leroux is forced to watch as his girlfriend, Sherrie White, is tortured on camera, under orders to not interfere, her continued suffering providing intel too valuable to sacrifice.

Black Widow (Book #5)

USA Today bestselling author J. Robert Kennedy serves up another heart-pounding thriller in Black Widow. After corrupt Russian agents sell deadly radioactive Cesium to Chechen terrorists, CIA Special Agent Dylan Kane is sent to infiltrate the ISIL terror cell suspected of purchasing it. Then all contact is lost.

J. ROBERT KENNEDY

Available Delta Force Unleashed Thrillers

Payback (Book #1)

The Vice President's daughter is kidnapped from an Ebola clinic, triggering an all-out effort to retrieve her by the elite Delta Force just hours after a senior government official from Sierra Leone is assassinated in a horrific terrorist attack while visiting the United States. As she battles impossible odds and struggles to prove her worth to her captors who have promised she will die, she's forced to make unthinkable decisions to not only try to save her own life, but those dying from one of the most vicious diseases known to mankind, all in the hopes an unleashed Delta Force can save her before her captors enact their horrific plan on an unsuspecting United States.

Infidels (Book #2)

When the elite Delta Force's Bravo Team is inserted into Yemen to rescue a kidnapped Saudi prince, they find more than they bargained for—a crate containing the Black Stone, stolen from Mecca the day before. Requesting instructions on how to proceed, they find themselves cut off and disavowed, left to survive with nothing but each other to rely upon.

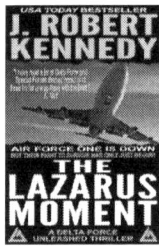

The Lazarus Moment (Book #3)

AIR FORCE ONE IS DOWN. BUT THEIR FIGHT TO SURVIVE HAS ONLY JUST BEGUN!

When Air Force One crashes in the jungles of Africa, it is up to America's elite Delta Force to save the survivors not only from rebels hell-bent on capturing the President, but Mother Nature herself.

Kill Chain (Book #4)

WILL A DESPERATE PRESIDENT RISK WAR TO SAVE HIS ONLY CHILD?

In South Korea, the President's daughter disappears aboard an automated bus carrying the spouses of the world's most powerful nations, hacked by an unknown enemy with an unknown agenda. In order to save all that remains of his family, the widower president unleashes America's elite Delta Force to save his daughter, yet the more they learn, the more the mystery deepens, witness upon witness declaring with certainty they never saw any kidnappers—only drones.

Forgotten (Book #5)

ONE OF THEIR OWN IS DEAD.
NOW IT'S TIME FOR REVENGE.

On a mission to rescue a young American woman held by ISIS as a sex slave, one of the Delta Force's Bravo Team is killed, betrayed by a mole within the Unit. As the team reels from the loss, the CIA presses hard to find the young woman and give the team a second chance to fulfill their mission. And seek revenge for the death of their comrade.

Available Detective Shakespeare Mysteries

Depraved Difference (Book #1)

SOMETIMES JUST WATCHING IS FATAL

When a young woman is brutally assaulted by two men on the subway, her cries for help fall on the deaf ears of onlookers too terrified to get involved, her misery ended with the crushing stomp of a steel-toed boot. A cellphone video of her vicious murder, callously released on the Internet, its popularity a testament to today's depraved society, serves as a trigger, pulled a year later, for a killer.

Tick Tock (Book #2)

SOMETIMES HELL IS OTHER PEOPLE

Crime Scene tech Frank Brata digs deep and finds the courage to ask his colleague, Sarah, out for coffee after work. Their good time turns into a nightmare when Frank wakes up the next morning covered in blood, with no recollection of what happened, and Sarah's body floating in the tub.

The Redeemer (Book #3)

SOMETIMES LIFE GIVES MURDER A SECOND
CHANCE

It was the case that destroyed Detective Justin Shakespeare's career, beginning a downward spiral of self-loathing and self-destruction lasting half a decade. And today things are only going to get worse. The Widow Rapist is free on a technicality, and it is up to Detective Shakespeare and his partner Amber Trace to find the evidence, five years cold, to put him back in prison before he strikes again.

Zander Varga, Vampire Detective

The Turned (Book #1)

Zander has relived his wife's death at the hands of vampires every day for almost three hundred years, his perfect memory a curse of becoming one of The Turned—infecting him their final heinous act after her murder. Nineteen year-old Sydney Winter knows Zander's secret, a secret preserved by the women in her family for four generations. But with her mother in a coma, she's thrust into the frontlines, ahead of her time, to fight side-by-side with Zander.

Made in the USA
Middletown, DE
07 November 2025

21041962R00179